Y0-BVQ-107

DO NOT REMOVE
CARDS FROM POCKET

Henry's
Special Delivery

Henry's Special Delivery

By M. C. Delaney

Illustrated by Lisa McCue

E. P. DUTTON   NEW YORK

Library of Congress Cataloging in Publication Data

Delaney, M. C. (Michael Clark)
 Henry's special delivery.

 Summary: Henry gets much more than he bargained for
when he sends for the panda offered on the back of a
cereal box.
 [1. Pandas—Fiction. 2. Humorous stories] I. McCue,
Lisa, ill. II. Title.
PZ7.D37319He 1984 [Fic] 83-27480
ISBN 0-525-44081-X

Published in the United States by E. P. Dutton, Inc.,
2 Park Avenue, New York, N.Y. 10016

Published simultaneously in Canada by
Fitzhenry & Whiteside Limited, Toronto

Editor: Julie Amper Designer: Isabel Warren-Lynch

Printed in the U.S.A. W First Edition
10 9 8 7 6 5 4 3 2 1

for Christine

The Package

One quiet, lovely Indian summer afternoon in November, a U.P.S. truck pulled up in front of the Whitfields' red house. A small man in a brown uniform hopped out. He walked to the rear of the truck, checked to make sure there were no unfriendly dogs around, and then opened the doors. He pulled out a package that was almost as big as he was, lugged it up to the Whitfields' front door, and rang the doorbell.

The U.P.S. man waited and waited. When almost a minute passed and still no one had come to the door, he rang again. This time Mrs. Whitfield, who was out in the backyard raking leaves, heard the doorbell. She hurried around the house to see who it was.

"Hello," she said, smiling.

"Package for Mr. Henry Whitfield," grunted the U.P.S. man.

"He's not here at the moment," said Mrs. Whitfield.

"He's not here?"

"He's in school."

"He's in school?"

The U.P.S. man looked as if he was about to faint. "This package weighs a ton," he said. "Where can I put it?"

"Oh, here, I'm sorry," said Mrs. Whitfield. "Please bring it inside." She held open the storm door for him.

In the front hallway, Mrs. Whitfield couldn't quite make up her mind where, exactly, to put the package. "Hmm. Let's see now. Should it go upstairs in Henry's bedroom . . . or would it be better in the TV room?"

The U.P.S. man finally decided for her. He lost his grip and the package slipped out of his hands, falling with a heavy thud onto the hall floor.

There was a loud "Oomph!"

"Oh, my goodness! Are you all right?"

"That wasn't me," replied the U.P.S. man, pulling out a handkerchief.

"That wasn't you?" asked Mrs. Whitfield.

The U.P.S. man wiped the perspiration from his brow. "Nope."

"Are you sure?"

"Positive."

"But I heard an 'Oomph.' "

"That wasn't me," he said. "That was the package."

Mrs. Whitfield stared at the U.P.S. man for a moment. "The package said 'Oomph'?" she asked him suspiciously.

"Well, not the package," cried the U.P.S. man impatiently. "Something *in* the package said 'Oomph.' "

At that moment, the package let out a great sneeze.

"See what I mean?" said the U.P.S. man. "There's something in there. Something *alive!*"

"Heavens!" exclaimed Mrs. Whitfield.

The U.P.S. man shook his head. "I'd sure like to know what's in there."

"Well, I'm afraid Henry won't be home till two thirty," said Mrs. Whitfield.

"Can't you open it?"

"But it's not mine."

"You're his mother, aren't ya?"

But Mrs. Whitfield was definitely not one of *those* mothers who go around opening their son's Special Delivery packages. "It's Henry's package," she said firmly. "And Henry will be the one who opens it."

The U.P.S. man rolled his eyes. "Well," he said. "I guess I can stick around for a while." And he sat down on the deacon bench in the front hallway.

"You can?" said Mrs. Whitfield, surprised, and sat down next to him.

The package sneezed again.

"I bet it's a bum," said the U.P.S. man. "I bet a bum with a bad cold mailed himself to your son. That's what *I* think."

Just then Henry walked in the door.

Homer

"Henry!" cried Mrs. Whitfield.

"Hi, Mom," said Henry. "Hey, whose package is that?"

Mrs. Whitfield looked at the U.P.S. man. "Henry, I'd like you to meet the U.P.S. man," she said politely.

The U.P.S. man stood up and smiled at Henry.

"Oh," said Henry. "I'm glad to meet you." He shook the U.P.S. man's hand.

"Aren't you going to open your package?" asked the U.P.S. man, patting the top of the box.

Henry's face lit up. "Oh, wow! You mean he's here!" he shouted. "I can't believe it! I just can't believe it! He's here! He's really here!"

"Who's here, dear?" asked his mother.

"The panda I sent away for," said Henry, signing for the package.

"A panda?" said Mrs. Whitfield.

"A panda?" repeated the U.P.S. man.

Henry reached into the pocket of his jeans and pulled out his Swiss Army knife. He snipped the rope that was tied around the package. His heart was beating wildly. It seemed like years had passed since he'd seen that Limited Time Only offer for a panda on the back of a box of his favorite kind of cereal. The panda had cost Henry a small fortune, plus two Proof-of-Purchase seals. But now here he was! Here he was—all the way from the Himalayas!

Unfortunately, Henry's mother wasn't quite as thrilled. "Who said you could get a panda?" she asked.

"Oh Mom, it's only a panda," said Henry. He ripped off the brown wrapping paper and carefully began to slit the masking tape on the cardboard box.

"Only a panda!" wailed Mrs. Whitfield. "That's easy for you to say, Henry Whitfield. You're not the one who'll wind up having to take care of it."

"You don't have to worry," replied Henry. "You're not going to have to take care of him."

"That's what you always say when you get a new pet. The truth is you'll feed him for two days and then guess who'll have to feed him? Me. That's who."

"You will not."

"Suppose he bites someone?" demanded Mrs. Whitfield. "Suppose he bites a delivery man? Then what?"

The U.P.S. man looked horrified. "Do pandas bite?" he asked. "You know, I really should get going. You wouldn't believe all the packages I have to deliver." He quickly let himself out of the house.

Mrs. Whitfield placed her hands on her hips. "Well, Henry Barrett Whitfield, there's going to be some mighty big trouble when your father gets home from work!" she announced fiercely, and then she stormed out of the house, slamming the door.

Henry bent down and finished slitting open the cardboard box. Then he slowly pulled up the flaps and looked in.

There, all scrunched up with a suitcase, was the panda. He was black and white and was wearing an old beat-up U.S. Army jacket. He didn't look at all like the picture on the back of the cereal box, which showed this cute little panda in a red striped T-shirt.

Shyly, Henry said, "Hello."

The panda stood up and groaned. He placed his paws on the small of his back and stretched.

Henry smiled. "My name is Henry Whitfield."

"I'm Al," said the panda, thrusting out his paw.

"Al," said Henry, as he shook the panda's big paw. He noticed that the panda was wearing an enormous silver I.D. bracelet around his left wrist.

"*Al*ka-Seltzer!" cried the panda, and broke up with laughter. "I'm only kidding. My name is really Pete."

"Pete?" said Henry.

"*Peat* moss!" shouted the panda, bursting into laughter again. "Just joking. Just joking. My name is really E."

"E?"

"*E*gads!"

Henry wondered how long this was going to go on. The panda finally got a hold of himself.

"My name is really Homer."

"Homer?" said Henry. "Homer what?"

"Just Homer," he said. "The owner gets to pick a

new last name." He sniffled. His eyes grew very moist. He sniffled again. "Ah . . . ah . . . ah . . . ah-chooooo!"

"Gesundheit!" exclaimed Henry.

"I have this terrible cold," explained Homer, sniffling.

"That's too bad," said Henry. He certainly was sorry to hear Homer wasn't feeling well. He was annoyed, too, that the cereal people had sent him a defective panda. He wondered if the thirty-day trial guarantee included pandas with terrible colds. Then he wondered what pandas take for colds. "Would you like a Kleenex?"

Homer shook his head. "I read somewhere that the best thing for a cold is a Scooter Pie."

"Really?" said Henry.

Homer nodded. "Yeah. I read it in *Newsweek* magazine. Ah-chooooo!" He looked at Henry desperately. "Quick!" he cried. "I need a Scooter Pie!"

"But we're all out!" said Henry frantically.

"What, no Scooter Pies!" exclaimed Homer.

"We have Twinkies?" said Henry.

"*Twinkies!*"

"Will they do?"

Homer raised his paw to indicate a sneeze coming on. "Ah . . . ah . . . ah . . . ah-chooooo! They'll have to," he said, sniffling, and picked up his suitcase. Sneezing, he followed Henry into the kitchen.

The Phone Call

After Homer had wolfed down the last three Twinkies, a peanut butter and grape jelly sandwich, and a couple of Oreo cookies and had gulped down a tall glass of chocolate milk (he was sure chocolate milk was much better for curing colds than plain old milk), Henry brought Homer upstairs to his bedroom—which wasn't quite as easy as it sounds. Anything that looked the least bit interesting, Homer stopped to investigate. There were the family photographs on the bookshelves in the TV room. ("Is that really *you?*" he wanted to know.) The bowling trophies on the living room fireplace mantlepiece. The sculpture Mrs. Whitfield had made of a dog on the staircase landing. ("What the heck *is* it?")

At the top of the stairs Homer looked in a doorway. "Whose room is this?"

"Sarah's—my little sister's," said Henry.

Homer spotted a small plastic incubator that was sitting in a slant of bright sunlight on Sarah's dresser, next to her Winnie-the-Pooh lamp. He went in to take a closer look at it. He peered into the incubator's domed transparent top. "What kind of eggs are these?"

"Quail. Sarah sent away for them from an ad she saw in one of my *Boys' Life*s."

"Really!" exclaimed Homer. "I'm an expert on eggs, you know."

"No, I didn't know."

Homer nodded. "I once hatched a dinosaur egg."

"You did!" said Henry. "What happened when it hatched?"

"I had to let it go."

Henry just stared at Homer.

When Homer entered Henry's bedroom, he took one look at all the rock posters and highway signs and old flags and neat ads that were on the walls, and cried, "What a great room!" He set his suitcase down and stepped up to a poster of Bruce Springsteen. "I have this poster, too," he said. He wandered around Henry's room, exploring. He checked out Henry's transistor radio, his walkie-talkies, his stereo system, his harmonica, his shortwave radio, his seashell collection, his autographed baseball of the 1982 New York Mets baseball team, his beer can collection, his small bronze replica of the Statue of Liberty.

"Er, listen, Homer," said Henry. "I've got something I've got to do. I'll be right back."

Homer was studying Henry's chameleon terrarium. "OK," he said.

Henry closed the bedroom door behind him, and walked quickly down to the end of the hall to his parents' room. Entering the sunny room, he quietly closed the door. He stepped over to the window and looked out into the backyard. His mother was standing by the swing set, raking leaves. She was raking the leaves into little piles—piles that later Henry and his older brother, George, would have to haul away into the woods. Even though the window was closed, he could hear the *scratch, scratch, scratch* of the rake. She was raking furiously—you could tell she was still really mad.

Henry left the window and walked over and sat down on his parents' bed to think. He had to mull things over. The truth was, Henry hadn't gotten the panda for himself but for Heather Callahan, a girl in his class. Heather Callahan loved pandas. She had pandas on practically everything she owned. She had pandas on her lunch box, textbook covers, pocketbook, wristwatch, shoelaces. Sometimes she wore a fuzzy pink sweater to school that had a bunch of pandas dancing across the front of it, and once, back in September, she had brought a stuffed panda bear into class. She was always drawing little pandas, too, in her loose-leaf notebook. Even the pencils she drew them with had pandas on them.

Yet even though Heather Callahan was in his class, Henry had never said a word to her. Not one word. He was too frightened. Not that he hadn't tried. Henry was always thinking of ways to strike up a conversation with her, but every time he was just about to speak to her, his heart would start to race and, trembling all over, he would chicken out.

That's why Henry was simply delighted when he saw the cereal box offer for the panda. He figured he could finally get to talk to Heather Callahan by giving her a panda. He had it all planned out how he was going to give her the panda, too. He'd go to school very early one morning and wait in the playground, near the bicycle racks. The moment Heather Callahan saw the panda, Henry knew she'd just flip out. She'd want to know where he got him and where she could get one, too. Henry would calmly answer all her questions, and then, very generously, he'd announce, "Tell you what. How would you like *this* panda?" If all went according to plan, this would, Henry hoped, make him very popular with Heather Callahan.

The only problem was there wasn't any school tomorrow on account of a big teachers' conference. Then, after that, it was Thanksgiving vacation. He wouldn't be seeing Heather Callahan again for almost a week, and it would be impossible to keep Homer hidden that long. Henry was terrified that if he kept the panda until Monday and then gave him to Heather Callahan, his family would all want to know what he'd done with the panda. "If anyone ever finds out I got a girl a panda," thought Henry, "I'll never hear the end of it." Boy would *that* be humiliating! He gazed forlornly at the phone that was sitting on the little night table beside the bed and sighed. "What am I going to do?" he groaned.

All of a sudden, Henry got this great idea. He pulled out the drawer of the night table and took out the telephone book. He turned to the C's, and found the

Callahan's number. He sat very still for almost a minute, collecting his courage. His insides felt all funny, the way they always did whenever he had to get up and speak before the entire class. He went over in his mind what he was going to say, then he picked up the receiver. As he was dialing the last digit, Henry abruptly hung up. He couldn't simply call Heather Callahan and say, "I got you a panda." She'd think he was a real weirdo. Henry sat staring at the phone. "I've got it," he thought. "I'll tell her, 'I got this panda in the mail today and he has a cold and I don't know what to do for him. You seem to know a lot about pandas, so I thought you might be able to help.' " This was perfect. Henry practiced this speech several times. Then he dialed the number again.

His heart thumped like crazy as the phone rang.

"Hello?" said a woman's voice.

"Hello," said Henry. He idly started fiddling with some of his mother's bobby pins that were lying on top of the night table. "Is Heather home?"

"Who's this?"

"Henry," he mumbled.

"Harry?"

"Henry," he said more clearly. Henry was so nervous he began to drop the bobby pins into his father's sneakers that were sitting on the floor alongside the bed. "You don't know me. I'm a friend of Heather's. Actually, I'm not really her friend. I'm just a kid in her class."

"Just a minute, Henry. I think she's up in her room."

Henry heard her set the phone down. Then he

heard her yell "Heather, telephone! It's Henry some-body-or-other!"

For what seemed like several years, Henry waited for Heather Callahan to come to the phone. What could be taking her so long? Henry could just see her coming all the way downstairs only to be terribly disappointed to find out that it was just *him* calling.

"Oh, this is a big mistake!" thought Henry misera-bly, and hung up. He felt so stupid.

When Henry returned to his bedroom, Homer was gone. Homer certainly hadn't wasted any time moving in—his stuff was all over the room. Henry sighed. He began to search the house for Homer. He finally found him in the backyard, talking to Mrs. Whitfield. Not only that, Homer was wearing one of Henry's father's old hats.

"Hello, Henry!" said Mrs. Whitfield. "Did you know that Homer once raked up a seventeen-foot pile of leaves?"

"Seventeen and a half," Homer corrected her.

Mrs. Whitfield shook her head in wonder. "Imag-ine! Seventeen and a half feet high! Why that's almost as big as our house! Homer is telling me all about the Himalayas. They sound just beautiful." Apparently, she wasn't angry anymore. She stopped raking sud-denly and looked at Henry in a peculiar way. "Don't you feel well, dear?" she asked him. "You look like you just lost your best friend."

"I'm fine."

Mrs. Whitfield felt his forehead. "You feel a little warm."

Henry said, "I'm OK, really."

"I have to pick your brother up from the Y later. Is there anything I can get you?"

Standing behind Mrs. Whitfield, Homer opened his mouth wide and began pointing into it. Then he pretended to sneeze.

"Oh," said Henry. "Could you buy some more Scooter Pies?"

The Who Am I Sweepstakes

That evening, before Mr. Whitfield came home from work, Henry warned Homer to keep out of sight.

"My dad will have a fit if he sees you," explained Henry. Actually, Henry wasn't so worried about his father having a fit as he was about what would happen if anyone discovered his real reason for getting Homer. "And if George and Sarah find out about you, they're likely to tell my dad. He can be pretty mean sometimes."

"He can?" blurted Homer.

Just then, there was a knock on Henry's bedroom door. Henry and Homer froze.

"Who's there?" asked Henry.

"Your father."

Henry and Homer stared at each other in horror. "Quick!" whispered Henry. "Get in the closet!"

Homer raced into the closet and closed the door behind him. Henry waited a moment, then opened his bedroom door a crack, and peeked out and saw his father. "Oh, hi, Dad!" Henry quickly stepped out into the hall, closing his door behind him. "How was work?"

"Terrible," grumbled his father.

"Oh!"

"I've got a splitting headache!"

"Oh!"

"And I'm going to throttle the next person who makes my day any worse. Now. I thought I asked you to empty the kitchen wastebasket when you got home from school this afternoon."

"Oh, yeah," said Henry. "I guess I forgot."

"Well. What are you waiting for?"

As his father was entering his bedroom to change out of his suit, Henry hurried downstairs to the kitchen, where he found his mother taking a meat loaf out of the oven.

"What did you do with Homer?" she asked. Wearing hot mitts, she set the tray of meat loaf down on the counter.

"Who?"

"Homer."

"Oh, the panda!" cried Henry. He removed the big wastebasket that was in the cabinet under the sink, and pulled out the plastic bag that was filled with garbage. "I sent him back."

His mother looked at him. "You sent him back?"

"Yeah," said Henry. He hated lying to his mother,

but he didn't know what else to do. "I just figured he'd be too much trouble to keep."

At that moment, a door suddenly slammed upstairs. Henry's heart stopped. His father had discovered Homer!

From the top of the upstairs hall, Mr. Whitfield hollered: "If I catch the person who's been putting bobby pins in my sneakers, I'll wring his neck!"

Mrs. Whitfield frowned at Henry, then shrugged. "I guess it's just as well you sent Homer back," she said. "I don't think this would've been such a great night to tell your father you got a panda."

Henry had absolutely no appetite at dinner that evening. At one point, his mother begged him to please eat *some*thing, dear, but Henry only replied, "I'm not very hungry." The problem was, he couldn't stop thinking about his phone call to Heather Callahan. He hated himself for being such a big chicken. He was also very worried about how he was going to keep Homer hidden. Not only was Henry not eating anything, he wasn't saying much, either. Nor for that matter was Mr. Whitfield, who was still in a grumpy mood.

George was telling the rest of his family about this terrific sweepstakes he had heard about on his favorite radio station.

"All you have to do is write a paragraph or two," said George.

"That's all?" asked Mrs. Whitfield. "What does it have to be about?"

"You," said George, mushing down his mash potatoes, which were quite lumpy. "I mean, me. I mean, it's got to be about yourself—the person who's writing it."

Mrs. Whitfield reached for her glass of milk. "Just a paragraph or two about yourself?" she said. "That sounds easy."

"It's the Who Am I Sweepstakes," said George informatively.

"I'm going to enter," announced Sarah. "Guess what I'm going to write about?"

"I don't know," said Mrs. Whitfield. "Your Thanksgiving play?"

"No. My quails!"

George finished his milk and set his glass down on the table. "You can't write about them," he said.

Sarah was up in arms at once. "Why not?"

"Because it's supposed to be about you," George said. "Not a bunch of stupid birds."

"They're not stupid!"

"Besides," said George, "they haven't even hatched yet."

Mrs. Whitfield laughed. "That's what you call counting your quails before they've hatched." She turned to Henry. "Why don't you enter the sweepstakes, too, Henry? And don't slouch, dear."

Henry sat up a little straighter in his chair. "I've got nothing to write about," he mumbled. He started to chop up his meat loaf.

"Face it, Henry," said George. "You just lead a very boring life. Mr. Dullsville."

Mrs. Whitfield leaped to Henry's defense. "That's

not true," she said. "Henry has lots of interesting things to say about himself."

"Like what?" asked George.

"Well, he almost won last year's Easter egg contest."

"Big deal," replied George. "Now take me. I can write that I'm a straight-A student, I can do sixty-three push-ups, I can beat anyone in a staring contest, I have a perfect attendance record, I've built two tree forts, I'm the sec—"

"Oh, Henry," Sarah broke in. "I know what I wanted to ask you. Could I borrow your fake ice cube with the fly in it?"

George looked very upset. "I beg your pardon, Sarah," he exclaimed crossly.

Sarah looked at him blankly. "What?"

"You're interrupting."

"I'm just asking Henry a question."

"I don't care," he said. "You're interrupting."

Sarah ignored him. "So," she said, turning toward Henry. "Could I please borrow it?"

"No," said Henry. "You'll only lose it."

"No, I won't," insisted Sarah. "I promise I won't."

George rolled his eyes. "I don't believe this!" he wailed. "I just don't believe this! I've never seen a family with such bad manners."

"Please can I borrow it?" begged Sarah. "I promise I'll take good care of it. I just want to play a joke on Debbie Hunsdorfer tomorrow. Please can I borrow it?"

"I said no, Sarah."

"Thanks a lot, Henry," said Sarah in a nasty voice. "Some brother you are!"

"All right," said Mr. Whitfield, losing his temper. "That's enough out of both of you!"

George rose with his empty glass and, walking over to the refrigerator, poured himself some more milk. After he sat down, he cleared his voice, the way teachers do when they're trying to get your attention—your *undivided* attention. "Now. As I was saying before I was so rudely interrupted." He glanced over at Sarah. "There's just no end to all the things I can write about myself for the Who Am I Sweepstakes. I can say that I'm the second fastest runner in the eighth grade, I can hold my breath for over a minute, I am distantly related to Calvin Coolidge, the thirtieth president of the United States, and I have thirty-eight dollars and sixty-three cents in the First National State Bank."

Mr. Whitfield suddenly put down his fork. "That's funny," he said.

Everyone looked at him. "What's so funny about that?" demanded George.

"Shhhh!" he whispered.

Mrs. Whitfield leaned forward.

"What is it, dear?" she whispered.

"I don't know," he said. "I thought I heard something."

"Uh-oh," said George, ominously.

"Shut up, George!" Mr. Whitfield told him.

Everyone sat very still, listening. Sarah inched away from the kitchen window.

21

All of a sudden, from upstairs, there was a loud sneeze.

Startled, everyone at the table jumped.

Mr. Whitfield looked at them with alarm. "What was *that?*" he whispered.

"It might be my radio," said Henry quickly.

"Your radio?" said his father.

"Yeah, I might've left it on," said Henry.

"*That* was your radio?" repeated Mr. Whitfield in disbelief.

Oddly enough, George, without even knowing it, came to Henry's rescue. "I bet they're having a sneezing contest," he said.

"A *sneezing* contest?" said Mr. Whitfield.

"Yeah," said George. "Last week they had a burping contest. You should've heard the guy who won. He was really something."

Mr. Whitfield gave them all a what'll-they-think-of-next look. Then he looked at Henry and said, "Next time make sure you turn off your radio before coming down to dinner, young man."

Henry promised he would and asked if he could please be excused from the table.

"But you haven't eaten a thing on your plate," said his father.

Henry looked down at his dinner. "I guess I'm not very hungry."

Mr. Whitfield sighed. "All right."

Henry got up from his chair and went into the pantry. He opened up the new box of Scooter Pies and took two out. On his way through the kitchen, Henry tried to hide the Scooter Pies, but his father spied them just the same.

"I thought you said you weren't hungry," Mr. Whitfield said to him.

"I'm not," replied Henry, and hurried out of the room.

Unable To Sleep

After dinner, Henry stayed up in his bedroom, with his door closed. While Homer (still with Mr. Whitfield's hat on), sat over in the beanbag chair listening to records on Henry's headphones and reading Henry's *Mad* magazines, Henry lay on his bed and examined a roadmap of his town that, some weeks ago, he had gotten from the glove compartment of the car. The map showed all the streets and highways and parks and bridges and woods and swamps and ponds and the enormous river in Henry's town. As he did almost every night, Henry liked to look at the line on the map that said Whippoorwill Road. Whippoorwill Road— *1620* Whippoorwill Road to be precise—was where the Callahans lived. The street was north of Henry's house, on the other side of the big river. Henry had circled Heather Callahan's street with a red Magic

Marker. That circled area was as magical as Disneyland to Henry. It made his spine tingle.

At around eight thirty, or maybe it was quarter to nine—at any rate, while the rest of the family was down in the TV room, watching some Thanksgiving special, Henry decided to sneak out of the house to go for a bicycle ride. Homer wasn't too keen about the idea. For one thing, as he pointed out to Henry, it was quite chilly out. It was also very dark. But Henry wanted to ride up to the top of Winding Ridge Road. That's because at the top of Winding Ridge Road there was a wonderful view of the entire town, which was especially pretty at night, when all the lights were lit up and the sky was peppered with sparkling stars.

As they pedaled up the hill, Homer, who was on George's ten-speed racer, could hardly keep up with Henry. "Are we almost at the top?" he asked, panting. He had no idea why they were bicycling up the hill.

Henry looked back at him. "Just about," he said and, leaning over his handlebars, pedaled harder.

When they reached the top of the hill, they were both out of breath. For almost a minute, they sat on their bicycles, looking at the town, gasping.

Homer finally said, "Hey, Henry."

Henry continued to stare down at the town. "Yeah?"

"I know this is going to sound stupid, but why did we come way up here?"

"I just wanted to look out at where a girl I know lives," said Henry.

"Oh, yeah?" said Homer, and looked at the town. "Which light is her house?"

26

"I don't know," replied Henry. "I think it's one of those lights way, way out there. She's out there somewhere."

"Let me guess," said Homer. "You got the hots for her."

"I do not," snapped Henry.

"Don't worry," said Homer. "I won't tell a soul."

It seemed like it was growing colder by the minute. Sniffling, Homer zipped up his army jacket. Then he cupped his paws together and blew into them to warm them up. "Sort of nippy out, don't you think?" he said.

Henry didn't get the hint. "Mmm," he replied.

Homer looked up at all the stars. "I hear we're in for a big frost tonight," he continued. "Sure feels like it, huh?"

"Mmm," said Henry.

Homer looked at him. "Geez, you must be freezing in just a sweatshirt."

"Mmm."

"I bet it's nice and cozy back in your bedroom."

"Mmm."

"I can just hear the radiator pipes banging and pinging away."

"Mmm."

"Hey, did you hear that?"

"What?" said Henry with a start.

"I thought I heard your mother yelling for you."

"You did?"

"I think so."

Henry said he thought they had better go then, and hopping back on their bicycles, they began to coast down the hill. A few minutes later, when they were again in Henry's warm bedroom, Henry went down-stairs to the TV room and casually asked his mother if she had been looking for him. She said no, she hadn't. When Henry returned to his bedroom and told Homer this, Homer replied, "Must've been some other Henry's mom, I guess."

That night, as usual, Henry stood outside the bath-room door, in his blue flannel pajamas with the little hunters on them, and waited for Sarah to come out. Every so often, to hurry Sarah along, he'd impatiently rap on the door, saying, "C'mon, Sarah, would ya hurry up!"

"I am!" snapped Sarah, who wasn't at all.

When Sarah, dressed in her peppermint-pink flannel nightgown, finally stepped out of the bathroom, Henry said, "Well, it's about time."

Sarah stuck her tongue out at him. Then she hopped down the stairs, like a Slinky.

The moment the coast was clear, Henry hurried over to his bedroom door, and gave the secret tap that he and Homer had agreed on. Homer came out, with his toilet kit under his arm. He was in blue pajamas with little people on them. The two of them dashed across the hall into the bathroom, and Henry closed the door. Homer took the guest sink, and Henry took the sink he always used. Homer pulled out a toothbrush and a tube of Crest from his toilet kit, and started to brush his teeth.

Removing his toothbrush from the toothbrush holder on the wall, Henry was about to run the toothbrush under cold water, when he saw something he'd never noticed before. There was an H and a C on the hot and cold water faucets.

"Hey, *H* is for Heather and *C* is for Callahan," Henry said to himself, perfectly delighted at his big discovery.

Then he brushed his teeth.

That night Henry couldn't sleep. Homer, on the other hand, slept like a log. He lay on the floor, curled up in Henry's sleeping bag, snoring.

With his hands clasped behind his head, Henry lay in bed, staring up at a stain on the ceiling. He kept thinking about Heather Callahan. He wished he had told her about Homer on the phone. "How am I ever going to hide Homer till next Monday?" Henry groaned.

He glanced at the alarm clock on his night table. The fluorescent hands said 3:12. Henry was sure he'd still be up when the sun rose.

Henry started thinking about a day last August, when he and his father drove to New Hampshire to pick George up from summer camp. As they were leaving the pinetree-shaded camp, George had turned to Henry sitting beside him in the front seat, and said, "Why didn't you write me?"

"I meant to" was all Henry could say.

George said nothing. But Henry could tell by the sad look on his face that it would've meant the world to George if he had sent him even just a postcard.

A terrible thought suddenly occurred to him.

"Suppose I die in my sleep or something," he thought. "Heather Callahan will never know I was going to give her Homer."

Henry couldn't stand it. He *had* to do *something*.

"I know. What if I delivered Homer to Heather Callahan myself? I could knock on her door and pretend I was lost or something. Then when she saw Homer and flipped out, I could just do what I was going to do at the playground at school." This was terrific. "But how would I get over there?" Henry thought hard. "Let's see. . . . I can't ask Mom to drive me over—she thinks I sent Homer back. Wait. Maybe Homer and I could bicycle over there. No, that won't work. Mom and Dad would come looking for me in the car. Or else they'd call the cops. We'd get caught in no time. Especially since we have to go over the bridge to get across the river." There was a police station by the bridge. "I suppose we could always walk. But we'd still have to go over the bridge. Unless . . . "

Henry sat up in bed. He had an idea. A great idea.

He sprang out of his bed, clicked on the lamp on the night table, and slipped into his clothes. Then, stepping over Homer, he went over to his closet and got out his knapsack, his tent, and George's sleeping bag that he'd borrowed and forgotten to return that time Wally Hunsdorfer slept over. He opened the flap on the knapsack, and stuffed in a couple of pairs of socks, a sweater, gloves, a pair of jeans, his walkie-talkies, his road map, his transistor radio (along with two new batteries he had in an old cigar box on his book shelf), a flashlight, and the $14.78 he had in his Snoopy bank on top of the dresser. He noticed as he was getting the money out of the bank that Homer's large silver I.D. bracelet and digital wristwatch were lying on top of the dresser. He picked up the bracelet and took a closer look at it. Engraved across the face of it, in big letters, was HOMER. He set the bracelet down.

Quietly, Henry sneaked downstairs to the kitchen. He snapped on the kitchen light and got out four cans of Coke and a jar of grape jelly from the refrigerator. He put them into a brown shopping bag he found in the cabinet with all the lunch boxes. Then he went into the pantry and, from the shelves, took down a bag of marshmallows, a half-eaten bag of Oreos, an opened box of frosted flakes, two Almond Joy bars, a jar of peanut butter, and a loaf of raisin bread. Hands full, he brought everything into the kitchen and placed it in the shopping bag. He pulled open the silverware drawer and removed two spoons, a fork, and a butter knife. He put them into the shopping bag, too, and then carried the bag upstairs to his bedroom. After he had packed all the stuff in his knapsack, he stood for a moment, thinking. Had he forgotten anything?

Homer suddenly snored. Yes, he'd forgotten one thing.

Henry crept back downstairs, and looked in the pantry for the new box of Scooter Pies.

They were gone!

Henry searched all over the kitchen for them. He looked everywhere. The bread box. The refrigerator. The cabinet where all the drinking glasses were kept.

31

Inside the oven. The liquor cabinet. All of a sudden, it dawned on him where they were. He returned upstairs, and as quietly as 007, he stole into Sarah's bedroom. Her door, as usual, was opened slightly, and the lamp by her bed was on.

Henry silently crossed the room and pulled open the top drawer of her dresser. He looked under her socks, where her Secret Hiding Place was. Sure enough, the box of Scooter Pies was there. Henry removed the box, put the socks back just the way he found them, and closed the drawer. He was about to leave, when his eye fell upon the incubator on top of the dresser.

The four quail eggs had hatched!

A thrill ran through Henry. They were so tiny! So cute and fluffy looking! He was so excited that, for a moment, he almost went over and woke Sarah to tell her. He tapped the domed top with his index finger.

"Hello," he whispered, smiling.

Henry walked across the room to the door. As he was closing the door behind him, he looked over at Sarah. She was sound asleep with her mouth open and her thumb not quite in her mouth. A notebook that she'd been drawing in was on the floor, opened. Henry went over and pulled up her covers. Then he kissed her on the cheek and snapped off her lamp.

Back in his own bedroom, Henry packed the box of Scooter Pies in his knapsack. Then he closed it up and tied George's sleeping bag to the aluminum frame. He went over to his desk, sat down, and, pulling open the top drawer, took out his compass. He set it down on the desk, by a bottle of India ink, and then dashed off the following note to his family.

Dear Mom and Dad and George and Sarah,
   There is something I must do, which can't wait another minute. It's too important. Please do not worry about me. I'll be OK.
                                        Much love,
                                        Henry

P.S. Sarah, the baby quails look really neat! And you can borrow my fake ice cube if you like. I think it's under the couch in the TV room.

P.P.S. If I'm not home in time for Thanksgiving, please say hello to Granny for me.

Henry placed the note on the center of his pillow. Then he woke Homer up.
   "Pssssst, Homer," he whispered.
   Homer didn't so much as stir.
   "Homer!"
   He still didn't wake.
   "Homer, would you wake up, for crying out loud!"
   Henry squatted and gave Homer a good hard shake. Even then he didn't wake up right away. Finally, though, he opened his eyes. Then, after a moment, he groaned.
   "What time is it?" he asked, drowsily.
   "Time to get up," said Henry. He began collecting Homer's things and putting them into his suitcase.

Homer closed his eyes.

"*Wake up!*" Henry ordered sharply.

Homer opened his eyes and sat up. "What's up?" he asked, yawning.

"Shhhhh!" whispered Henry. "Hurry up and get dressed. We're going on an expedition."

Homer groaned and slowly got up to dress. Clearly, he would much rather have stayed in bed.

Setting Out

Lugging his suitcase, Homer followed Henry into the chilly, dark garage. "What's the big rush?" he asked.

"Shhhh," said Henry, snapping on the garage light. "Not so loud."

"What's the big rush?" whispered Homer.

"I'll tell you later," he said.

Henry set down his knapsack and got down the aluminum stepladder from where it hung on the wall alongside the rakes, shovels, pickax, hoe, crowbar. He carried it over to the shelves that were in front of the Toyota, climbed up the ladder, and started to hand things down to Homer. An old deflated rubber inner tube. A yellow beach pail. A toy tugboat. A beach umbrella. A lawn chair. Another lawn chair. Finally, Henry found what he was looking for: a little blue plastic boat, a varnished wooden paddle, and two pumpkin-orange life preservers.

After he had put everything back on the shelves and returned the stepladder, Henry unlocked the garage door and, very slowly (for he knew it creaked like crazy), lifted it up. When Henry and Homer had finished putting all their stuff into the boat, Henry picked up the bow and Homer lifted up the transom, and together, they carried the boat out of the garage and set it down on the driveway.

There were millions of stars out, and all the houses in the neighborhood were dark and silent. It was freezing. In the moonlight, the lawn was silver with frost, and you could see your breath. Henry got his gloves out of his knapsack and put them on, and then lifted up the hood of his ADIRONDACK MTS. sweatshirt. Homer slipped on a pair of mittens he had in his suitcase, and zipped up his army jacket. After folding up his collar, Homer pulled out Mr. Whitfield's old hat from the pocket of his jacket, and put that on.

Henry was all set to pull down the garage door, when he remembered how much noise it made, and changed his mind. So, instead, he just snapped off the garage light. The two of them returned to their places by the boat and, on three, lifted it up and lugged it across the back lawn. Every few feet, they kept running into the small leaf piles that Henry's mother had raked up the day before. There was a woods just behind Henry's house, with a path that began by the old doghouse. At the edge of the back lawn, they got on the path and followed it through the woods until they came to a power line which, in the ghostly light of the full moon, was overgrown with tall, dried grasses.

Enormous steel-beam towers that held up high-tension wires stood, awesomely, along the power line.

Homer suddenly stopped.

"What's the matter?" asked Henry, turning around.

Homer sniffled. "Ah . . . ah . . . ah . . . ah-choooooooooo!" he sneezed.

"Gesundheit!" said Henry.

"Ah . . . ah . . . ah . . . ah-choooooooooo!" sneezed Homer again.

They set the boat down and Henry got out the box of Scooter Pies from his knapsack. He gave one to Homer.

"Ah, just what the doctor ordered," said Homer, and went over and sat down on an old, crumbled stone wall that stood near the power line. "So," he said, tearing open the cellophane wrapper on the Scooter Pie. "Tell me about this big expedition."

Henry sat down beside him. "There's not much to tell, really," he said. "We're going to see the girl I was telling you about last night."

"But I thought she lives really far away," said Homer, taking a bite of his Scooter Pie.

"She does. We'll just have to get there. That's all."

"So why the boat?"

"We need the boat to cross the river," said Henry.

Homer looked at him. "What river?"

"The river we have to cross."

"Wait a minute. You didn't say anything about a river," said Homer. "You just said we were going on an expedition."

"It's part of the expedition."

38

"Some expedition," replied Homer. "Why can't we just take the bridge?"

"The bridge?"

"Yeah, isn't there a bridge?"

"It's way out of our way," explained Henry. "Besides, we'd have to go on all these streets where we're likely to be seen."

"Well, all I can say is, I better not fall into the river. I have a bad cold, you know."

"If I were you," said Henry, "I'd be more worried about what's on the other side of the river."

"Why? What's on the other side?"

"Monsters."

Homer stared at him. "Monsters?"

"From outer space."

Homer abruptly leaped up, strode over to the boat, grabbed his suitcase, and started to walk back the way they'd come. "See you later," he yelled, without even turning around.

Henry stood up. "Where are you going?" he called.

"Back."

"Look, Homer. There probably aren't any monsters," Henry said quickly. "My brother told me that, and he was probably just making it up."

"Well I don't want to be the one to find out," replied Homer.

Henry hurried after him. "But you can't go back. You're my panda!"

Homer kept right on walking. "Who says?"

"I sent away for you, and you have to do what I say."

"Okay," said Homer. "You win." He stopped and swung around. "But I'm not getting mixed up with any monsters. No sirree, Bob. And that's final."

Henry and Homer walked back to the boat.

"Boy are you lucky," said Henry. "Now I don't have to eat your candy bar."

Homer's eyes lit up. "You mean you've got candy bars? So where's mine?" he said, holding out his paw.

"Not until we reach the river," said Henry, and bent down to pick up the boat.

On the River

The sun was just coming up when they arrived at the grassy shore of the river. A smoky mist was curling up from the water. They set the boat down, and Henry unpacked the Almond Joys. They sat down on an old stump and ate the candy bars. Then Henry took everything out of the boat, and dragged it down to the edge of the water. Rising, Homer crunched his candy bar wrapper up into a little ball and tossed it into the woods. He picked up the paddle and, shouting "Heads up!" to Henry, heaved it down by the boat. Then he tossed down the two life preservers. He was just about to chuck Henry's knapsack, too, when Henry cried out in alarm, "Don't throw that!"

Homer laughed. "I'm only fooling." He picked up his suitcase and carried it and Henry's knapsack down to the boat.

Henry helped Homer on with his life preserver.

"You get in first," he said to Homer, fastening the strap.

Homer said, "Oh, no, I wouldn't hear of it. After you."

"No, I think you should get in first," said Henry.

"I insist, though," exclaimed Homer, sounding like a perfect gentleman. "After *you.*" He bowed, holding out his paw.

"All right, if you say so," said Henry as he put on his life preserver. "I just thought you'd rather sit up in the bow and look at the scenery. But if you'd rather do all the work and paddle, well—"

"On second thought," said Homer, "perhaps I would like to get in first."

He got in and sat down in the bow. After Henry handed Homer all their gear, he squeezed into what little room was left. He picked up the paddle to push the boat off the side of the bank. They were stuck fast. Standing up, he stepped into the water. It was ice cold. The muddy bottom, which was all yucky, oozed up between his toes. Henry pushed the boat off, then gingerly hopped in.

The moment he did, the boat sank so low, it nearly capsized.

"You really must go on a diet, Henry," said Homer. He leaned over the side of the gunnels; when he did, water almost came gushing into the boat.

"Don't do that!" Henry shouted in alarm. "Want us to go under or something? There's way too much weight in the boat."

"Want me to throw over your knapsack?" asked Homer.

"But it's got all the food in it."

"Yikes! It does?" cried Homer, and hugged the knapsack to his chest. "Well, I guess you'll just have to swim it, Henry."

"*Me?*"

"Don't forget I have a bad cold."

"We'll have to go back," said Henry, and paddled the boat to shore.

Henry hopped out and pulled the boat up onto the bank, and then Homer stepped out with the knapsack and suitcase. He sat down on a large rock and watched as Henry paced back and forth along the bank. "What'll we do now?" wailed Henry, forlornly. "How will we ever get over to the other side?"

"Maybe we could build a bridge," suggested Homer.

"That would take too long," replied Henry, miserably.

"Well, how about if we build a tunnel? We could call it the Homer Memorial Tunnel, and we could charge seventy-five cent fares to cross. You and I could switch off being toll collectors." Homer was growing more excited by the second. He suddenly leaped up and started for the woods.

"Where are you going?" Henry called after him.

"To look for a couple of good digging sticks," said Homer, and disappeared into the woods.

Henry was seated on the bank, glumly throwing pebbles into the water and watching them form rings, when he heard the creak of oars. A moment later,

Homer came around the bend, rowing a boat. Henry thought he was seeing things.

Homer grinned. "Need a lift, sonny?" he called.

Henry sprang to his feet. "Where the heck did you find that?"

"Down the river."

"Whose is it?"

"Got me," replied Homer, rowing the boat in toward shore.

Henry grabbed the bow. "Do you think we should take it?"

"Would you rather we build a tunnel?"

Henry jumped in, and Homer rowed out into the river. He looked around at Henry. "Where to, boss?"

"Home, James," said Henry, smiling.

The sky was an ash gray and the mist was steaming up all around them from the river. As Homer rowed, Henry watched the shore grow smaller and smaller. Although Henry had been to the river hundreds of times with George to catch tadpoles and frogs, he'd never actually gone out onto the river in a boat. The shore looked neat from the river, with all the bare tree branches hanging over the water. With the mist, it looked really spooky. Henry sort of wished George could've been there, too, to see it. They were about halfway across, when a man stepped out of the woods, down the river a ways. You could barely see him through the cold, rising mist.

The man raced down to the edge of the river. "Hey!" he yelled at them. "Come back here with my boat!"

Homer stopped rowing and looked up. "Uh-oh," he said. The boat instantly began to drift with the current.

Henry whispered, "What should we do?"

"I'll keep rowing and pretend I didn't hear him," said Homer. He started to row again.

"Hey, you two!" shouted the man, fiercely. "Give me back my boat!"

"We'd better go back," said Henry.

Homer swung around and looked at him. "Why?" he demanded. "We're safe way out here. What can he do? Nothing."

"Yeah, but it's his boat," said Henry.

"So?"

"So, we can't take his boat," continued Henry. "That would be stealing."

Homer hesitated. For a brief moment, he looked as though he were about to argue the point, but then sighing, he shook his head. Resignedly, he turned the boat around and headed back to shore.

"What do you think you're doing taking my boat?" cried the man. "I ought to have you both arrested."

"We're really sor—" Henry started to say, when Homer, turning around in his seat, punched him in the leg.

"*Arrest us?*" cried Homer, looking terribly innocent. "All we were doing, sir, was rescuing your boat."

The man looked confused. "Rescuing my boat? You mean it floated away?"

Homer pointed to Henry. "If it wasn't for Horatio, here, your boat would be about ten miles down the river by now."

The man looked at Henry, and Henry smiled shyly.

The man noticed Henry's bare feet. They were all wet. His jeans were still rolled up to his knees. "I guess I owe you fellas an apology," he said.

"Oh, no, don't thank me," said Homer. "Horatio's the one you should thank."

The man turned to Henry. "Thanks a million, Horatio." He shook Henry's hand. "I wish I could return the favor."

Homer said, "Well, you know, maybe you can."

Both the man and Henry looked at Homer. "I can?" said the man.

"Well, you see, we were on the other side of the river when Hen—*Horatio*—jumped in after your boat. Maybe you could give us a ride back to the other side."

"Why, I'd be delighted to," cried the man. He placed his hand on Henry's shoulder. "Hop in, Horatio, my boy!"

"Thanks," said Henry.

The man turned and started to walk up the bank. "I'll be right back," he said, and disappeared into the woods. A few seconds later, he reappeared, lugging a lawn statue of a jockey holding a latern.

"What's that?" asked Henry.

"This is my buddy, Jackson," said the man. He set the heavy lawn statue down in the boat so that it was standing up. "I never go anywhere without him."

Pushing the boat off the bank, the man waded out into the river with the boat. Then he climbed in. Homer, surrendering the thwart to him, moved to the stern. The man picked up the oars and began to row. He rowed a thousand times better than Homer.

Henry, putting on his socks and sneakers, was

studying the lawn statue. "You know," he said, tying his shoelaces, "our next door neighbors have a statue just like Jackson in their front yard."

The man looked at him in surprise. "No!"

Henry nodded.

The man shook his head. "I tell you," he said, "everyone's got one now."

"The Spendjians' statue even has its thumb broken off—just like this one." He pointed to the lawn statue's broken thumb.

"Isn't that amazing!" exclaimed the man.

"I'm not kidding," said Henry. "You should see the Spendjians' statue. It looks just like this one."

"That's really something," replied the man. "What a coincidence."

When they reached the opposite shore, the man helped Henry and Homer take their gear out of the boat. "I wonder if you guys would do me a big favor," he said.

"Sure," said Henry and Homer together.

"Don't tell anyone you saw me."

Henry asked, "How come?"

"I just like to keep a low profile," said the man. "That's all."

Both Henry and Homer promised they wouldn't tell a soul. The man thanked them, and then headed out onto the river.

"Boy, are you gullible," Homer said to Henry, as they watched the man disappear into the mist.

Henry looked at him. "What?"

"You know that statue?"

"Yeah."

"That *was* your next door neighbors'."

Henry opened his eyes wide. "Oh, my gosh!"

"What?"

"*I* shook hands with him!" exclaimed Henry in horror. He stared down at his hand as though it were contaminated.

Swindled!

In a nice little clearing a short ways from the river, Henry and Homer sat down on a rotten old log and, with the warm sun shining upon them, had a perfectly delicious breakfast of Cokes and marshmallows.

"I guess anything can happen now," remarked Henry, popping a marshmallow into his mouth.

"Tell me about these monsters from outer space," said Homer.

"Well, George says they're very ugly," replied Henry.

"Yikes!"

"So ugly, people faint," continued Henry. "But only grown-ups. Not kids."

"How about pandas?"

"I don't know about pandas."

"Where are they?"

"I don't know. I suppose they could be anywhere."

"*Anywhere?*" repeated Homer, nervously, looking around.

"That is, if they really exist," replied Henry. "My brother tends to lie a lot." He took his walkie-talkies out of his knapsack, and handed one to Homer, saying, "Take this. Just in case . . ."

Homer pulled up the antenna and clicked on the on button. All he picked up, however, was static. He turned it off, put the antenna down, and hung the walkie-talkie around his shoulder.

The sun, hot and bright, had burned off the fog and was now fairly high up over the bare treetops. It was going to be another beautiful Indian summer day. Homer unzipped his army jacket. Henry pulled off his sweatshirt. He dug his hand into his pocket for his compass.

It was gone!

"Hey!" he cried.

"What?" said Homer.

Henry searched his other pockets. "I can't find my compass," he replied.

"Does that mean the expedition's off?" asked Homer, hopefully.

"I wonder if I lost it?" said Henry. He knelt down and began to fumble through his knapsack for it. "What did I do with it?" He glanced at Homer. "Wait a second! You don't suppose that guy with the boat stole it, do you? I mean, maybe he was also a pickpocket or something. You never know."

"I tell ya, Henry. I think we ought to turn back,"

said Homer. "We might get really lost without a compass."

"I bet I know where it is!" exclaimed Henry. "I bet you anything I left it on my desk." He tossed his knapsack over in disgust and sat back down on the log. "Oh, brother! Now what are we going to do? We won't know what direction to go in."

"Honestly, Henry. I really think we ought to turn back."

"What time do you have?" asked Henry.

Homer looked at his digital wristwatch. "Seventeen minutes after nine."

"Well, they must've found my note by now," said Henry. "I sure hope my Mom doesn't worry too much. She worries a lot."

"We can always skip the expedition, you know, Henry," suggested Homer again. "I mean, if you're really worried about your mom."

"No," said Henry. "Let's get going."

"Ah . . . ah . . . ah . . . ah-choooooooooo! Ah . . . ah . . . ah . . . ah-choooooooooo!"

Henry got out a Scooter Pie for Homer.

"So tell me. What direction do we have to go in?" asked Homer, taking a bite of the Scooter Pie. "I mean, north, south, east or west?"

"North," replied Henry.

Homer swallowed. "Then we have to go this way." He pointed straight behind him.

Henry was very skeptical. "Now how do you know that?"

"See the moss on this log," said Homer. "Moss only grows on the north side of things."

Henry was just delighted. "I didn't know you knew stuff like that!"

"I read it in the encyclopedia," explained Homer. "I once read all the volumes of the *Encyclopaedia Britannica* in one sitting."

Henry stared at him in amazement. "You're kidding! How long did *that* take you?"

"I don't know. An hour or so."

"An *hour!*"

"I took a speed-reading course," said Homer, modestly.

Henry and Homer walked through a big woods and a meadow and more woods and a swampy place and up hills and down hills and over logs, and once they had to leap across a rushing stream. To make sure they were heading north, Henry always kept a sharp eye out for trees and logs with moss growing on them. Once, though, he spotted an old tree that had moss growing all around its trunk.

"Are you positive moss only grows on the north side of things?" he asked Homer.

"Would I steer you wrong?" Homer replied.

At around ten thirty or so, Homer was explaining how he happened to get mixed up with the cereal box offer, and got sent over to Henry.

"It's really a pretty crazy story," Homer was saying as he walked behind Henry. "One day I was at the barbershop and you know how sometimes you have to wait a million years before it's your turn to get a haircut?"

"Yeah."

"Well, it was one of those times. So, anyway, there I was reading a *Popular Mechanics* when I saw an ad that said Be a Pet and Make Up to $12 an Hour. Well, it sounded great. It really did. I mean, it sounded like all you did all day was sleep, eat, and get petted and hugged. I figured I'd give it a try for a while and see what happened. So, I took their training course, and the next thing I knew I was all wrapped up on my way to you."

"That's amazing!" exclaimed Henry. "You mean, you're making twelve dollars an hour right now?"

"Heck no," said Homer. "Only monkeys make that much. I don't know how much I'm making exactly, but it's around—Wait a second. *You're* supposed to know how much I'm making."

"Me?" said Henry.

"Yeah, you're the one who's paying me. . . . *Aren't* you?"

Henry shook his head. "First I've heard of it. The back of the box of the cereal box didn't say anything about that."

Homer stopped. "Oh, my gosh!" he wailed.

Henry turned and looked at him. "What's the matter?"

"I've been swindled!"

"You're kidding!"

"I wish I was," he said. "I knew something like this was going to happen. I just knew it. What a sucker I am. Geez, when will I ever learn? Well, I guess I can go home now."

"Home?" said Henry. "I hate to tell you this,

Homer. But according to my contract, you're under a lifetime guarantee."

"I'm what!" Homer cried. "Ah . . . ah . . . ah . . . ah-choooooo! Ah . . . ah . . . ah . . . ah-choooooo!"

Henry quickly got out another Scooter Pie.

Homer all but inhaled it. "Oh, brother," he moaned. "How do I get myself into these things?"

Henry felt badly for him. "I'm sorry."

"It's not your fault," replied Homer. "I'm always getting myself into messes like this. It could be worse. At least you're not a bad owner. I mean, hey, I could've gotten stuck with some old geezer." Homer sighed. "I just wish I'd brought along my record collection. I've got a huge record collection."

"Oh, yeah?"

"I belong to this record club that sends me all these great records. Well, that's not always true. Every once in a while, they send me a crummy one. You know, like *Joe Shmoe's Greatest Hits*. I just give those records to Bolt. He thinks they're terrific. He doesn't know any better. I wonder what old Nut and Bolt are up to?"

"Who're Nut and Bolt?" asked Henry.

"My buddies. They're a couple of lunatics. I should send them a postcard. Did I tell you I collect tacky postcards?"

Henry stopped. He was having trouble finding the path. "No," he said absently.

"Well, I do."

"What time do you have?" asked Henry.

Homer looked at his wristwatch. It's eleven o'-clock."

Henry started walking again.

Homer followed. "What was I saying again?"

"You were telling me about your tacky postcard collection."

"Oh, yeah," said Homer. "I really should send Nut and Bolt a postcard. Remind me to send them one, OK?"

"OK."

"Thanks," said Homer. "Geez, I wonder what those guys are up to? Probably no good. Nut's always getting expelled from school."

"Really?"

"Yeah. The three of us are in a rock band. I play drums. We practice in my garage."

"Do you hold concerts?" asked Henry.

"Oh, sure," replied Homer. "We play all over the Himalayas. Have you ever heard of Paul McCartney?"

"Of course."

"He once saw us and then came backstage and personally asked me to play in his band."

"No!"

"Yeah, he did. Really. I couldn't do it, though."

Henry swung around. *"Why not?"*

"I had school. Boy, do I miss those guys. I bet this very minute they're out throwing dummies in front of cars." Homer suddenly groaned. "Geez, my feet hurt. Don't yours?"

"Not really," said Henry.

"By the way," said Homer, "what's on the lunch menu today?"

"Peanut butter and jelly sandwiches."

57

"Sounds delicious," said Homer. "Aren't *you* starving? I certainly am hungry."

"We just ate."

Homer abruptly stopped. He began to wheeze.

Henry stopped and turned around to look at Homer. "Are you OK?" he asked.

"I think so," said Homer. He sniffled. He sounded just terrible. "Ah . . . ah . . . ah . . . ah-choooooooooo!"

"Gesundheit!" said Henry.

"Ah . . . ah . . . ah . . . ah-choooooooooo!" sneezed Homer again.

"Gesundheit!" said Henry again.

Homer kept sniffling.

Henry sighed. "Do you want to have lunch?" he asked.

Homer set down his suitcase. "I thought you'd never ask," he replied, grinning.

An Exclusive Interview

That afternoon Henry and Homer continued on their expedition. The scary thing was, Henry had no idea, really, where they were. He didn't dare tell Homer that, though.

They were both pooped when, at a little after three, they came to a small pond that was covered with lily pads. Henry, unslinging his knapsack, said, "This looks like a good spot to camp."

Homer dropped his suitcase. "Boy, am I beat!" he cried, flopping down on the ground. "My feet are killing me!"

After they had set up the tent and laid out their sleeping bags, side by side, Henry took out his transistor radio and flashlight from his knapsack and placed them between their sleeping bags. It was getting kind of chilly, so he put on his sweatshirt.

When Homer saw that peanut butter and grape jelly sandwiches were for dinner, he made a face. He groaned. "If I eat one more peanut butter and jelly sandwich, I'll croak," he announced. "Can't we have pizza tonight?"

"It's either peanut butter and jelly sandwiches," said Henry, "or nothing. That's all I brought along."

Homer somehow forced himself to eat two more sandwiches and split another one with Henry.

After dinner, while darkness was gathering in the woods and on the pond, Henry and Homer just took it easy inside the tent. Henry sat on George's sleeping bag, studying the map with his flashlight, while Homer, lying on Henry's sleeping bag, kept fiddling with the radio dial.

"This is WJMK, your New York City country radio station, 12.4 on the AM dial," said a man with a Texas twang. There was the *khrkhrkhrkhrkhr* of static. "Hello. What's your favorite radio station?" asked a man who talked very, very fast. "WMOL!" cried a girl. "You just won the new Hall and Oates album!" said the man. . . . *Khrkhrkhrkhrkhr* . . . "On the day that you were born the angels got together and decided to create a dream come true," sang The Carpenters. . . . *Khrkhrkhrkhrkhr* . . . *eeeeee*—"This has been a test of the Emergency Broadcasting System," said a man in a sober voice. "Had this been an actual emergency, you would have been instruct—" . . . *Khrkhrkhr* . . . "Sunny and unseasonably mild tomorrow with a high in the upper sixties," reported a woman cheerfully. "Right now, it's five thirty music time, and 64 WSGD degrees!" . . . *Khrkhrkhrkhrkhr* . . . "With ten seconds

remaining on the clock," cried a sportscaster, enthusiastically, "Syracuse University will go to the foul line."
. . . *Khrkhrkhrkhrkhr* . . . "Big girls don't cry-yi-yi," sang the Four Seasons . . . *Khrkhrkhrkhrkhr* . . . "For a dynamite white smile, and dynamite fresh breath," said a man, "Ultrabrite will get you noticed." . . . *Khrkhrkhrkhrkhr* . . . "We have an exclusive interview made earlier today on the front lawn of the Whitfields' house with George and Sarah—" a newscaster was saying, when Homer turned the station.

"Hey!" cried Henry. "Turn it back. That's my brother and sister!"

Homer found the station again.

" . . . of the boy who disappeared early this morning from his home," exclaimed a reporter now. "Tell me, George, where do you think Henry is?"

"You mean this very minute?"

"Yes."

"According to my calculations, he's out on the Atlantic Ocean, about fifteen miles off the shore of Nantucket."

"What makes you say that?" asked the reporter.

"Well, after we discovered that Henry was missing this morning, I made a quick but thorough search of the entire house."

"I looked, too," said Sarah.

"Would you please let me handle this, Sarah," George told her, impatiently. "As I was saying, I found that Henry had taken the jar of peanut butter and a loaf of raisin bread and the jar of grape jelly and a few cans of Coke and three Almond Joys—"

"I only took two!" declared Henry.

61

"And a bag of marshmallows and a box of frosted flakes—"

"We have frosted flakes?" inquired Homer, and began looking for the box in Henry's knapsack.

"And the rest of the bag of Oreos and the—"

"The Scooter Pies," piped up Sarah.

"And the Scooter Pies," repeated George.

All of a sudden Sarah started to cry. "I miss Henry," she said. "I wish he was home."

"Shhh," George said to her, gently. "He'll be OK, Sarah. Really. Listen, why don't you go inside? I'll be in in a minute." There was a pause, then George cleared his throat. "So, anyway, along with all these things, Henry took our little blue plastic boat that we take with us every summer when we go up to the Adirondacks. It's a really neat boat. You can paddle out in it to the middle of the lake, but you have to be careful that a big motorboat doesn't drive by too closely or its wake will swamp you. You'd really love the lake we go to in the Adirondacks," said George. "It's surrounded by all these big mountains and pine trees that smell just wonderful in the hot morning sun and—"

"You were saying about Henry," interrupted the reporter.

"Who? Oh, Henry! Well, my guess is, he's out in our little blue plastic boat, sailing across the Atlantic Ocean," stated George.

"Why do you think that?"

"Well, last night at supper I told everyone how I was going to enter the Who Am I Sweepstakes that this radio station is doing. Anyway, my mom asked Henry what he would write about if he were going to write something about himself, since to enter the sweepstakes you have to write a paragraph or two about yourself and send it to this radio station with a self-addressed stamped envelope and—"

"You were saying about Henry," interrupted the reporter.

"Oh, yeah. So, anyway, Mom asked Henry what he would say about himself and Henry couldn't think of a darn thing."

"That stupid jerk!" Henry blurted out. He sure hoped Heather Callahan wasn't listening. "I swear, I'm going to kill him when I get home."

"So," continued George. "All this has led me to believe that, since he has enough provisions to last a week and since he took our little blue plastic boat, Henry is sailing across the Atlantic Ocean for England so he can have something to write about for the Who Am I Sweepstakes."

"Thank you very much, George," said the reporter, "for the exclusive interview. From the Whitfields' front lawn, this is Ed Pendleton for WACR news—"

"Wait!" cried George. "I'm not through yet! I'd just like to add that, in case I'm wrong, I'm offering a reward of thirty-eight dollars and sixty-three cents to anyone with information on Henry's whereabouts—"

Henry reached over and clicked off the transistor radio. "How humiliating!" he moaned. "Now everybody thinks I'm out on the Atlantic Ocean looking for something to write about. That stupid George!"

"What are you talking about? That's terrific!" cried Homer. "Man! Nobody would ever put up that kind of money for me!"

"They wouldn't?" said Henry, who was feeling rather badly now that he had gotten mad at George.

"Are you kidding?" exclaimed Homer. "Think *my* brother would do something like that?" Homer shook his head. "Forget it. He's too busy building model battleships. I bet Roy doesn't even know I'm gone."

Henry looked at him with surprise. "I didn't know you had a brother, Homer."

Homer pulled out his wallet from the pocket of his army jacket. He flipped it open to all the photographs. "Here," he said, holding it so that it was practically in Henry's face. "This is a picture of him."

It was a snapshot of a panda in his bathing suit, waterskiing. Homer turned over the plastic transparent leaf. "And this is Roy in his Little League uniform," Homer went on enthusiastically. "He's not at all like me. I mean, I'm OK on a skateboard, but Roy's amazing. He's such a great athlete."

Henry looked up from the photograph. "What position does he play?"

"Catcher," answered Homer. "He's really excellent, too. The Boston Red Sox sent a scout to the Himalayas just to see Roy play."

"Wow!"

"Oh, here's Nut and Bolt," said Homer, turning to the next photograph. It was a snapshot of two pandas, mugging it up for the camera.

"And this is my mom and dad." Homer showed him

a snapshot of two pandas, with their arms around each other, standing before a picnic table.

Henry asked, "Where was this taken?"

Homer examined the photograph. "Yellowstone National Park. We went there on vacation the summer before last." Homer stared blankly at the snapshot. It was as if he were unable to go on to the next picture.

Henry felt a little sorry for him. He got out a Scooter Pie and handed it to Homer.

Finally, Homer flipped over the plastic leaf. He broke into a smile. "Here," he said. "This is my little sister."

The panda in the photograph looked just like a werewolf. "Gosh, she's ugly!" blurted out Henry without thinking.

Homer laughed. "I'm only kidding. It's really a picture of a werewolf." He pulled out a crumpled card and handed it to Henry.

"What's this?"

"My draft card."

Henry looked at him. "You've got a draft card?" he said, surprised. He'd sort of assumed that he and Homer were about the same age.

"It's fake," confessed Homer. "Looks pretty real, though, huh?"

"I'll say."

"And this is my official membership card to the Alfred E. Newman fan club," he said, handing Henry another card.

"Hey, I was going to send away for one of those."

"And this is my American Express card."

Henry was shocked. "You've got your own credit card!" he exclaimed.

"I never leave home without it," answered Homer casually. "Besides, it's expired."

"Want to see my pictures?" said Henry, and pulled out his own wallet. He flipped to a snapshot of an Irish setter.

"This is Jake," he said.

"I don't believe I saw him," said Homer.

"That's because he ran away about a year ago," replied Henry, flipping over the plastic leaf. "And this is my brother— Oh, and here's my mom and dad."

"Who took this picture?" asked Homer. "It's all blurry."

"Me," mumbled Henry, and quickly turned to the next photograph. It showed Sarah, pouting, with her thumb in her mouth.

Homer looked closely. "Hey, she's cute!" he exclaimed. "What's she like?"

"I don't know. . . . She's a little shy. She's always drawing."

"She go out with anybody?"

"She's only seven and a half!"

"So? My girl friend back home is only six."

"Do you miss your family much?" asked Henry quickly to change the subject.

Homer looked at Henry as though he'd just been terribly insulted. "What do you think I am, a little baby or something? Listen, you're talking to someone who is a real pro at living out of a suitcase."

"Well, I'm certainly glad to hear that," replied Henry. "I was kind of afraid you might get homesick if you had to spend the rest of your life with Heather Callahan."

"What!"

"You'll probably be spending the rest of your life with Heather Callahan. I'm giving you to her as a present."

"This is a joke, right?"

Henry shook his head. "No."

"But . . ."

"What?"

"The rest of my *life?*"

"I thought you said you were a pro at living away from home."

"Well, I am. But, geez. I just thought I was going to be *your* panda. I mean, we make such a good team and everything. I don't *want* to be owned by somebody else." Henry looked at Homer with sympathy. He was about to get him another Scooter Pie when he saw that he still hadn't finished his first one. "Eat your Scooter Pie," he said, gently.

"What?" replied Homer blankly.

"Eat your Scooter Pie."

"Oh." He looked at it for a moment without much interest, then held it out for Henry. "I'm not too hungry. You want it?"

Henry shook his head. "No thanks."

"I'll save it, then," said Homer, and put it into the pocket of his army jacket. For nearly a minute, Homer just sat there, staring dully before him. Then he said, "Hey, Henry, what if we sent away for another panda to give Heather Callahan?"

"Another one?"

"Yeah, we can give her another panda, and I'll go home and stay with you."

"But I can't afford another panda."

"You can't?"

"No."

"Oh," said Homer, and fell silent. After a minute, he slowly got up. . . . "I guess I'll go down to the pond and brush my teeth."

Henry handed him the flashlight, and Homer crawled out of the tent, leaving Henry in the darkness.

Henry got ready for bed. He pulled off his sweatshirt, kicked off his sneakers, and got into his sleeping bag. It had been a long day and he was exhausted. He closed his eyes, and thought about Homer's reaction to having to spend the rest of his life with Heather Callahan. Then he thought about George putting up all that reward money. What a great brother!

All of a sudden Henry heard something that made his heart stop. About ten feet away, over in the woods, a twig snapped. Then something started to shuffle through the dry leaves, crunching them up. It stopped. Henry sat bolt upright and stuck his head out of the tent. He looked all around him, but even with the bright moonlight, he couldn't see anything. He wished he had the flashlight with him.

"Homer?" Henry called out, nervously. "Homer, is that you?"

There was only the lonely sound of wind in the trees. Henry's heart was racing. He scrambled out of the tent and grabbed a stick to defend himself.

The shuffling started up again, and then, eerily, it abruptly stopped.

"Who's there?" demanded Henry. He was scared to death. He took a step back. He was all set to make a dash for it.

Suddenly, something enormous leaped out from behind a tree, crying, "Rrrrrraaaarrrgggh!"

Henry nearly died of fright.

It was Homer.

"Don't do that!" snapped Henry. His voice was shaking.

"Did you think I was a monster?" asked Homer excitedly, turning on the flashlight.

"I didn't know who you were."

"You should've seen your face."

"Very funny."

"Tell me the truth. Did you think I was a monster?"

"I told you. I didn't know who it was."

"Really," said Homer. "Did you think I was a monster?"

After Henry calmed down a bit and Homer stopped asking "Did you think I was a monster," they crawled back into the tent and climbed into their sleeping bags. Henry watched as Homer took off his hat, then undid his large silver bracelet.

"Where did you get that, anyway?" asked Henry sleepily.

Homer held up the bracelet. "This?" He looked at the bracelet admiringly. "My girl friend gave it to me."

Henry nodded. He yawned. Even though it was only around seven thirty or so, he could scarcely keep his eyes open. He told Homer, "I think I'm going to sleep."

Homer, however, said he thought he'd do some

reading before going to sleep. He got out something called *The Story Of A Bad Boy*, a book he'd borrowed from Henry's book shelf. He'd only read a couple of pages, when, looking up, he said to Henry, "What do you think your chances are of winning the Who Am I Sweepstakes?"

But Henry was fast asleep.

Returning to his book, Homer read for a few minutes more, then he closed the book and switched off the flashlight. Lying back, he felt something hard beneath his sleeping bag. He turned on the flashlight again to see what it was. His walkie-talkie. Just out of curiosity, Homer pulled up the antenna and clicked it on.

Static.

He pressed the transmitting button. "This is Homer signing off for the day," he said. Then he listened. Just static. A moment later, Homer was fast asleep.

About ten minutes after Homer had dozed off, the cackling static that was coming over the walkie-talkie speaker abruptly stopped. Two strange voices came on the walkie-talkie.

"Where are we?" asked one voice.

"I don't know," said the other voice.

"What'll we do?"

"Got me."

The voices came in loud and clear—whoever or whatever they were, they were extremely close-by.

Problems

Sometime in the middle of the night, Henry, who was a light sleeper, awoke. He lay still, listening.

"This just can't be right," a strange voice was saying over Homer's walkie-talkie.

Henry sat up and woke Homer.

"Whaaaa?" mumbled Homer sleepily, and rolled over.

"Homer, I heard somebody," whispered Henry.

Homer turned around and looked at Henry. "What are you talking about?"

Henry showed him the walkie-talkie. "Listen," he said.

"Are you sure this is right?" asked the strange voice again over the walkie-talkie.

"Of course I'm sure," answered the other voice.

Homer was wide awake now. "The monsters!" he whispered.

"I don't know who it is," said Henry.

"This certainly is a dumb game," remarked the first voice over the walkie-talkie.

"Oh, stop complaining, and *play!*" the other voice said.

"We've got problems," said Henry. "Big problems! We can't let anyone see us. Otherwise we might get caught."

"Whoever it is," said Homer, "they sound close. Real close."

Henry made a face. "I know. I know." He scrambled out of his sleeping bag and quickly put on his sneakers and sweatshirt.

"I wonder where they are?" asked Homer as he got out of his sleeping bag.

"I'll climb a tree," said Henry. "Maybe I'll be able to see something." He unzipped the tent flaps and crawled out. "Wait for me," cried Homer, rushing out of the tent after him. He wasn't about to be left alone in the tent. Not with monsters around.

Henry stepped up to a tree that had lots of good climbing branches and, with a boost from Homer, grabbed the lowest branch. He scampered up the tree as fast as a squirrel.

"See anything?" asked Homer in a loud whisper when Henry reached the top. Homer seemed extremely uneasy about being on the ground all by himself. "Don't stay up there too long, Henry. I'd hate to have you fall or something."

From his branch, Henry had a great view of the woods and the pond. He looked all around. "I don't see anything," he called down to Homer. He was about to come down when, on the other side of the pond, just beyond a hill, he spotted a yellowish light flickering softly. He could just make out the vague shape of a spaceship.

"Wait! There's a light!" he cried, pointing. "Oh, my gosh! I think it *is* the monsters! You know what this means?" he asked excitedly, as he climbed down from the tree.

"What?"

"We get to see real live monsters from outer space!"

"Henry, please tell me you're kidding."

"No, really, Homer. Just think about it. How many kids have seen real live monsters from outer space?"

Homer looked up toward the starry sky. "Why me?" he moaned.

After they had packed up all their stuff, they set out, with Henry leading the way. He carried the flashlight in one hand, his Swiss Army knife in the other. Homer carried his suitcase in one paw, a big, heavy-duty stick in the other, just in case he had to clunk one of the monsters over the head.

Neither one of them spoke—they were too afraid the monsters might hear them.

When they arrived at the back of the hill where Henry had seen the light, Henry snapped off the flashlight. "Be really quiet," he whispered to Homer. They started silently up the hill.

Homer clung even tighter to his big stick.

When they were almost at the top of the hill, Henry suddenly froze.

"What's the matter?" whispered Homer in a terrified voice.

"Listen!"

The strange voices they had heard over the walkie-talkie were chattering away just over the hill—but now they were talking to one another in a weird foreign language.

Henry slipped off his knapsack and Homer set down his suitcase. "Stay here," whispered Henry. Being as quiet as possible, he cautiously crept up to a tree. Then another. And another. And another. He peered around it.

At the edge of a golf course sat a small spaceship, throbbing with yellow and orange lights. It looked sort of like Sarah's incubator, only it was much larger. It had booster rockets and a ramp that led down to the grass. The spaceship had all these ribbons and funny-looking symbols written on it. A few feet away from the spaceship, over by the eighteenth hole, two little green monsters were playing golf. The monsters were not only extremely ugly, they didn't seem too bright, either. They were both holding their golf clubs by the putter ends.

Henry motioned to Homer.

"Holy moly!" exclaimed Homer when he saw the monsters. "Boy, are they ugly! They don't look too tough, though."

"Wait'll I tell everyone," said Henry, kneeling down. "They'll never believe me."

"Too bad we don't have a camera."

"You know what I'm thinking," said Henry.

"I'm scared to ask," replied Homer.

"Let's capture one."

"That's what I was afraid you were going to say."

"No, really, Homer. If we caught one, I'd be the only kid in New Jersey who ever caught a monster from outer space, I bet. Just think. George could write about me, too, when he enters the Who Am I Sweepstakes."

"I yi-yi," groaned Homer. "Say it ain't so."

"We need a plan," said Henry.

"I know what we'll do," said Homer.

"What?"

"We'll scare them."

"How do you scare a monster?"

"Look. They're not from earth, right?"

"So?"

"So, they don't know what's lurking around in the woods. For all they know, there might be other monsters. If they start hearing strange noises, they might be scared out of their wits and beat it."

Henry asked, "You really think so?"

"No, but it's worth a try."

"What should we do?"

"OK," said Homer. "Here's the plan. You sneak down closer to the golf course, and wait. I'll creep around to the back of the spaceship with the flashlight. When I flash two times, start shuffling your feet in the leaves. And groan, too. That should scare them into the spaceship. When they make a run for the ramp, I'll jump out from behind the ramp and grab one of them."

"What if they have weapons?" asked Henry, handing Homer the flashlight.

"I guess we're goners."

"Do you have your walkie-talkie on you?" asked Henry.

Homer patted the walkie-talkie hanging from his shoulder. "Right here."

"In case it doesn't work out and we get split up," said Henry, "I'll try to reach you on the walkie-talkie." Henry took a deep breath. "Well. Here goes." He stood up.

"Henry," said Homer, rising.

Henry looked at him.

"Nothing," said Homer.

"What?"

"Well, just in case for some reason, you know, just in case we never see each other again— Well, it's been real."

Henry couldn't think of anything good to say, so he said what his grandfather always said to him whenever they were saying goodbye. "Don't do anything I wouldn't do."

Homer nodded. Then he began to make his way down the back of the hill and into the darkness.

Henry stole down to the golf course. He hid behind a big tree to wait for Homer's signal. The monsters were just a few feet from him, jabbering away. They had no idea he was there. His heart thumped like crazy.

A Monster Honeymoon

The moment Henry saw the beam from the flash-light, over behind the spaceship, flash two times, he started to shuffle his feet in the dry leaves.

"Oooooohhhhhhhh!" he groaned.

The two monsters abruptly stopped talking and, dropping their golf clubs, looked up.

"Oooooohhhhhhhh!" Henry continued to groan, shuffling his feet.

One of the monsters began to look around, sniffing the air.

"Oooooohhhhhhhh!"

The monsters, appearing alarmed, began saying things to each other—but in that strange tongue.

"Oooooohhhhhhhh!" Henry kept on groaning. He was having a real blast. He noisily shuffled toward them, groaning, "Oooooohhhhhhhh!"

All of a sudden a very weird thing happened. The monsters changed colors, like chameleons. They changed from green to brown to yellow to blue to a bright red. Then they began to puff up their bodies. They puffed and puffed until they were twice the size they were before. This made them look ten times uglier. The monsters spun around and, waddling, made a beeline for the ramp on the spaceship. Henry watched in horror as Homer, hiding behind the ramp, suddenly leaped out in front of the monsters. Homer started to yell, "Rrrrraaaaaarrrhhhh!" but, in the middle of his yell, he saw how enormous the monsters had become, and horrified, he screamed: "*Yaaaaaaaaaaaa!*"

The monsters were just as shocked to see Homer. "*Yaaaaaaaaaaaa!*" they screamed.

Homer fainted.

Henry raced out onto the golf course, yelling, "Rrrrraaaaaaaarrrhhhh!"

The monsters took one look at Henry, screamed, and fainted. Instantly, they shrank back to their original size and turned green again.

Henry found himself standing over an unconscious panda and two unconscious monsters.

"Ohhhh," groaned Homer, coming to.

Henry, who was all out of breath, knelt down beside Homer. "Hey, Homer, we did it!" he cried, excitedly. "We scared them! We really scared them!"

Homer lifted his head up and looked over at the monsters. "I don't believe it," he said. "It worked!" He got up and walked over to them. "They must've been really terrified of us."

79

"You mean me," Henry told him.

"*You?*" cried Homer.

"Yeah," said Henry. "It was me who made them faint."

"That's because I scared them first," explained Homer. "After I scared them, anything could've made them faint."

"Get out of here!"

"It's true!"

"You just don't want to admit I'm a better scarer than you."

"You can't scare worth beans," snorted Homer.

"Wanna bet?" cried Henry. He made his ugliest face, and groaned, "Ooooooohhhhhhhh!"

Homer only laughed. "You call *that* scary?" He scrunched up his face, crossed his eyes, and moaned, "Uhhhhhhhhh!"

It was, admittedly, a pretty scary face. Henry screwed up his face even more. "Uhhhhhhhhh!" he groaned.

"Uhhhhhhhhhhh!" moaned Homer. He began to walk around like a hunchback, swinging his arms.

"Uhhhhhhhhhh!"

"Uhhhhhhhhhhhhh!"

Henry was about to groan again when, out of the corner of his eye, he suddenly saw something move. It was the monsters. They had awakened and were trying to sneak away.

"The monsters!" screamed Henry at the top of his lungs, and sprinted after them.

"I'll get this side," shouted Homer. He ran to the other side of the green, so they couldn't escape.

The second the monsters saw that they'd been spotted, they sprang up and, terrified, scampered under the spaceship. Henry ran over to the spaceship and got down on his hands and knees. "Where's the flashlight?" he cried to Homer, gasping for breath.

Homer looked. It was lying on the grass by the ramp where he had fainted. He picked it up, walked over and, squatting, handed it to Henry. Henry shone the flashlight beam on the monsters. They were stooped over, cowering under the spaceship. They looked petrified. Their enormous eyes were filled with fear.

"They must really think we're monsters," said Henry.

Homer glanced up at the spaceship door. "Hey, Henry," he said, standing up. "I think I'll go for a spin in my new spaceship." He walked over to the ramp.

Henry continued to look at the monsters. He felt sort of sorry for them. They looked so timid, so helpless. "You don't have to be afraid," he said, gently, to the monsters. "I won't hurt you."

Homer, stepping onto the ramp, stopped and stared at Henry in disbelief.

"Come on," coaxed Henry. "Don't be afraid. No one's going to hurt you."

"What are you doing?" Homer wanted to know.

"I'm trying to get them to come out," answered Henry.

Homer rolled his eyes. "You think they're really going to come to you?"

Henry ignored him. "Don't be afraid," he said to the monsters, in his softest voice. "I'm not going to capture you. Honest."

"Henry, for crying out loud!" said Homer. "They can't understand a word you're saying."

"I wish we had something we could give them," remarked Henry, who was thinking of the time his mother had used a pan of milk to coax a terrified kitten out from under a pricker bush.

"Like what?"

"I don't know," replied Henry. "What do monsters like?"

"Maybe there's something in the spaceship," said Homer. He walked up the ramp.

Henry tried speaking to the monsters again. "Don't be afraid." He held out his hand. "It's OK. Really."

Homer stopped at the top of the ramp and stuck his head in the doorway. "Man!" he cried excitedly. "You should see the inside of this thing!"

Henry looked up at him. "What's it look like?"

"There's millions of dials and switches and things," reported Homer. He disappeared into the spaceship.

Henry, turning, looked at the monsters again. "Come on," he said to them, kindly. "It's OK. Why are you so scared?"

The monsters just stared at Henry with their big, frightened eyes.

Homer reappeared at the top of the ramp, holding something that looked like a road map. "You should see all the strange maps of the universe they've got," he told Henry. "Look. I'm going to be in the spaceship, investigating. Maybe it would be a good idea to put our walkie-talkies on. So, if they suddenly attack you or something, you can call me for help."

Henry didn't really think he had too much to worry

about, but he pulled his walkie-talkie out from the pocket of his sweat shirt anyway, and turned it on. Homer switched his on. "Come in, Homer," said Henry into his walkie-talkie. "Over."

When Henry spoke, both monsters looked up with a start.

Henry cried, "*Hey!*"

"What?" exclaimed Homer in alarm. He hurried down off the ramp and came over and squatted beside Henry.

"Talk into your walkie-talkie," instructed Henry.

"I'm in the mood for love," sang Homer, horsing around, into the walkie-talkie.

But nothing happened.

"That's funny," said Henry. He pressed the TALK button on his walkie-talkie and said, "Hello."

Both monsters looked at each other in surprise. Then one of them said something unintelligible.

"*Hello!*" a strange voice said over both walkie-talkies.

It was one of the voices they had heard on their walkie-talkies before.

"Hello," said Henry again into his walkie-talkie.

The monster garbled something.

"Hello!" the same strange voice said again over the two walkie-talkies.

Henry's face lit up. "Did you hear that?" he exclaimed. "They can understand us over the walkie-talkies! We can talk to them now!"

"Let me talk to them this time," said Homer. "How are ya?" he said into his walkie-talkie.

Nothing happened.

He gave it another try. "Hey, monsters, what's cooking?"

Still nothing. For some reason, the monsters couldn't seem to hear Homer.

Homer looked very disappointed. "How come they can't hear me?" he wanted to know.

Henry shrugged. "Got me." He spoke into his walkie-talkie again. "Hello," he said. "My name is Henry."

The same monster who had spoken before said something else in gibberish.

"Hello, Henry," said his voice over the walkie-talkie.

"And this is Homer," said Henry into his walkie-talkie, patting Homer on the back.

Homer smiled and waved.

"You don't have to be afraid," went on Henry into his walkie-talkie. "Honest."

The monster garbled something.

"You won't hurt us?"

Henry shook his head. "No. You can come out. It's OK. Really."

The monsters hesitated, and then crawled out from under the spaceship. Henry and Homer stood up and took a step backward. The monster who was doing all the talking put his long ugly arm around the other monster and spoke.

"We're Mr. and Mrs. 11135-00128, Jr.,"

The other monster spoke then. "We just got married."

Then her husband spoke. "We're on our honeymoon."

"Well!" exclaimed Henry, delighted. "Congratulations!"

He stuck out his hand to shake hands with the monsters. Startled, the monsters backed away in fright. But then, when they saw it was OK, they both lightly shook hands with Henry. Homer, on the other hand, kept his paws at his side. Apparently, he wasn't about to touch a monster's slimy hand.

Mr. 11135-00128 spoke again.

"We're lost," his voice said over the walkie-talkies. "We're looking for the Milky Way."

"You're in the Milky Way," said Henry.

The monsters looked surprised. "Golf Land is in the Milky Way?" asked Mr. 11135-00128, incredulously.

"Golf Land?"

"Isn't this Golf Land?" he asked. He pointed across the fairway. "The sign over there says: GOLF LAND. That is, assuming I translated it correctly."

"That's the name of the golf course," explained Henry into his walkie-talkie. "You're on the planet Earth."

The two monsters looked at each other in astonishment. "*Earth!*" they cried together.

"How did we ever get on Earth?" asked Mrs. 11135-00128.

Her husband shrugged. "I must've taken a wrong turn," he confessed.

"Great!" she said, rolling her big eyes.

Mr. 11135-00128 looked at Henry. "We've got reservations at the Alpha Centurian Hide-A-Way." He took out a brochure from his pocket and, opening it, read to them about the Alpha Centurian Hide-A-

Way. "Located in the heart of the scenic Southern Sky," he said, "our motel is in the breathtaking Centaurus constellation." He looked up impressively at them.

His wife added, "We've reserved their little honeymoon cottage."

The two monsters looked lovingly at each other.

Homer suddenly remembered the map he had in his paw. "Here's a map," he said to Henry. "Maybe we can find it." He laid the map on the grass, and Henry shone the flashlight on it.

After studying the map for a minute, Henry found Earth and showed the monsters where, precisely, they were.

"Here's the planet the Alpha Centurian Hide-A-Way is on," said Mr. 11135-00128, pointing to a dot. It looked as though it were about a million miles away. "Let's see," he said, examining the map. "If we take the Aurora Borealis Freeway south and then get on Internebulae M-81, going west, that should get us there." He folded up the map.

Henry asked, "How long will that take?"

"Well, if we don't hit any rush-hour traffic or construction, we should be there by tomorrow evening," replied Mr. 11135-00128. "It's only around four and a half light-years away."

"Wow!" cried Henry in amazement.

Homer tapped Henry on the arm. "Ask them why they can't hear me."

"Homer wants to know why you can't hear him," said Henry into his walkie-talkie.

"What?" asked Mr. 11135-00128.

"Why can't Homer talk to you, too?" asked Henry. "Why can you only hear me?"

The monster thought for a moment. "It must be your heart," he answered decisively.

"My heart?"

"Yes, you must have a very big heart. You see, you can do anything with your heart. Watch," said Mr. 11135-00128, boastfully, and closed his eyes to concentrate. "OK, Henry. Now I want you to think of something."

Henry began to think of his compass. Nothing seemed to happen.

Mr. 11135-00128 opened his eyes.

"That's what you get for showing off," his wife told him.

The monster shrugged. "Well, almost anything."

The monsters said good-bye to Henry and Homer and returned to their spaceship. The ramp automatically slipped into the spaceship and the doors slid closed by themselves. Then the booster rockets fired, and the spaceship lifted up, slowly, into the air, with its lights swirling. All of a sudden there was an enormous blast, and the spaceship zipped off, disappearing into the pink dawn sky. If you had blinked, you would have missed it—that's how quick the spaceship was.

Staring up at the spot where the spaceship had vanished, Henry put his hands into his pockets.

"Hey, my compass!" cried Henry. "Now how did *that* get there?"

Missing!

After the monsters left, Henry and Homer went and collected their things from the woods. It was still very early as they walked across the fairway. The sun was coming up behind them, and their shadows, long and thin, slanted across the frosted grass. You could see your breath in the crisp air, but the sky was quite blue and you could just tell that, after the sun warmed things up a bit, it was going to be a nice day.

"What time do you have?" asked Henry.

Homer looked at this wristwatch. "Ten after seven," he said.

"You hungry?"

"I'm starving!"

"If we see a diner or something, we'll stop and have breakfast," said Henry, who was also starving. All that scaring had built up quite an appetite.

Homer said, "You know, I've been thinking."

"About what?"

"I don't think I should enter the Who Am I Sweepstakes."

"Oh, no?"

Homer shook his head. "Naaa. It's not fair to all the other kids."

"Why not?"

"They wouldn't stand a chance against me. I've done so much, you know."

"You have?"

"Sure. I'd like to give another kid a chance. Some poor kid who never wins anything. Like you."

"Me?"

"Sure, why not?" said Homer. "You can write about meeting the monsters, and when you win, you can use the prize money to buy another panda to give to Heather Callahan and I can go on being your panda."

"Aw, I'd never win."

"What do you mean?" demanded Homer. "Didn't you just hear me? I just said I'm not going to enter."

At the end of the fairway, they came to some tennis courts, with nets that threw long cobwebby shadows upon the red clay courts. There was a clubhouse by the tennis courts and by the clubhouse was a telephone booth. As they passed the clubhouse, Homer stepped into the telephone booth to see if anyone had forgotten his money in the change return. No one had. Instead of coming straight out, Homer just stood there, staring at the telephone.

When Henry realized Homer wasn't behind him, he turned and called, "Hey, what's up?"

Homer stepped out of the phone booth, with a peculiar look on his face.

"What's the matter?" asked Henry, worriedly.

"Ah . . . ah . . . ah . . . ah-choooooooooo!" sneezed Homer. "Nothing," he said, sniffling. "I was just thinking."

"About what?"

"Well, I was just thinking I really should give my folks a call."

Henry was awfully anxious to get going. "It's kind of early," he said, trying to discourage the idea. He started walking. "Wouldn't they still be sleeping?"

"I don't know," answered Homer, following him. "They're in a different time zone."

"If you really want to you can call them," said Henry, without conviction.

"Naaa. That's OK."

Henry stopped and looked at Homer. "Listen," he said, "why *don't* you give them a call. They'd probably love to hear from you."

"I don't have any money."

"I've got some."

"You do?" said Homer. But then he shook his head. "Ah, it'd probably cost a mint."

"So what?" said Henry. "I've got loads of change." He slipped off his knapsack, unzipped one of the outside compartments, and took out all the quarters and dimes and nickels and pennies that were inside. "Here," he said, handing the money to Homer.

"How much is this?"

"Fourteen dollars and seventy-eight cents," said Henry. "You won't be able to talk for long, but you'll get to say hello."

They walked back to the phone booth, and Homer, slipping a dime into the coin slot, dialed O.

"I'll wait over here," said Henry, and started walking toward a bench by the clubhouse.

Henry noticed a bundle of newspapers lying by the clubhouse door, and went over to take a look at the top paper. He nearly died when he saw the front page.

MISSING! blared the headline.

And there, under the headline, was a huge black-and-white photograph of Henry, smiling.

"Oh, no," moaned Henry. "I'm famous."

It was a rotten photograph of him, too—that one the school photographer took of him last year, which showed him with his ears sticking way out. Henry pulled out his pocketknife and snipped the rope that was holding the newspapers together. He pulled out a paper and read the caption under his photograph.

Discovered missing from his home early yesterday morning, Henry Whitfield is feared to have drowned. Story on page 5.

"*Drowned!*" cried Henry in horror. He flipped to page 5, and saw a photograph of his boat pulled up on the river bank.

The caption under the photograph said: *Henry Whitfield's little blue plastic boat was discovered late yesterday afternoon on the bank of the river behind the Whitfields' house. Police believe the boy took the boat out onto the river and fell overboard.*

There was another photograph alongside it that

showed Henry's father, dressed in his business suit, diving into the river.

After rushing home from his office, Ernest Whitfield, the boy's father, leaps into the river to help police divers search for Henry's body, said the caption.

Henry began to read the story.

Nov. 24. A twelve-year-old boy was discovered missing from his home early yesterday morning by his mother, police report. The boy, Henry Whitfield, is the son of Mr. and Mrs. Ernest Whitfield, of 160 Woodbine Circle. Police believe the boy left his home sometime before five o'clock Tuesday morning. A little blue plastic boat owned by the Whitfields was found, abandoned, on the shore of the river behind the Whitfields' house late yesterday afternoon by a neighbor looking for a missing lawn statue. No reason was given by either the police or the family as to why the boy took the boat out onto the river at such an early hour.

The boy, police believe, fell out of the boat and drowned. As of eleven o'clock last night, no body was found. Police say they will continue searching the river today.

After Henry had read the article, he just sat on the bench, numb. It certainly felt strange to be dead. He felt like crying. He didn't know what to do.

Henry suddenly heard an "Ah . . . ah . . . ah . . . ah-chooooooooo!" He looked over at the phone booth. Homer had just stepped out of the phone booth and was standing there, about to sneeze again. Henry quickly looked in his knapsack and pulled out the box of Scooter Pies. There was only one left. He folded the newspaper, and tucked it into his knapsack. After tossing the empty Scooter Pie box into a nearby garbage can, he hurried over to give Homer the Scooter Pie.

Homer gobbled it down in two seconds. "Any more?" he asked, hopefully.

"That was the last one," said Henry. "Did you get hold of your folks?"

Homer shook his head. "It was busy. Roy's probably talking to his girl friend or something." He gave Henry back his money. "Are you OK? You look terrible."

"I just have to make a quick phone call," said Henry and stepped into the phone booth. He put a dime into the coin slot, and then dialed his home.

His mother answered on the first ring. "Hello?"

"Hi, Mom, it's me, Henry. I'm not dead, so please don't worry," he said, and hung up.

House of Pancakes

On the other side of Golf Land, they came to a quiet road. Henry examined his compass and headed north. Homer started to walk along the white line in the middle of the road, and Henry came over to walk beside him.

After a mile or so, they came to a busy highway that was loaded with all kinds of places to eat and motor lodges and gasoline stations and miniature golf courses and car dealerships and department stores. There was a McDonald's, a Stereo Warehouse, a Furniture City, a Lamp Town, a Burger King, a Bowl-o-Mat, a Cake Land, a Carpet World, a Danceorama, a Mr. Muffler, a Play Land, a Cinema City, a U-Fill-It gasoline station, which was right across the street from a Fill-Em-Fast gasoline station, which was on the opposite corner of a Y-Pay-More? gasoline station, which was directly across the street from an E-Z-Fill-Er-Up gasoline station. And just past that, was the House of Pancakes.

A waitress with menus under her arm greeted them the moment they walked in the door.

"How many?" she asked.

"Two," answered Henry.

The waitress looked at Homer. "No pets are allowed in the restaurant," she said.

"I beg your pardon!" exclaimed Homer, deeply offended. "But Henry is not a pet!"

The waitress looked all confused. "I'm terribly sorry," she apologized. She led them to a booth way in the back of the restaurant that looked out on the rear of the parking lot, where all the kitchen garbage cans stood.

"Hey, *some* view!" said Homer, as he sat down.

The waitress handed each of them a menu, then went and got them each a glass of water.

Homer studied the menu. "What are you having?" he asked Henry.

"I don't know," replied Henry. Everything looked so expensive.

"I think I'm going to have twelve blueberry pancakes, a sweet roll, and a tall glass of orange juice." He closed the menu and looked at Henry. "How about you?"

Henry was frantically trying to add up in his head the cost of Homer's order. Around eleven dollars! He closed his menu. "I don't know. I'm not very hungry."

Homer stared at him in disbelief. "You're not hungry?" he cried. "How can you not be hungry?"

Henry shrugged. "I'm just not."

"Man, I'm starved!"

The waitress came back. "Are you ready to order yet?" she asked, looking at Henry.

Henry turned away. He was worried she might recognize him from his picture in the newspaper. "You go first," he told Homer.

"I'll have twelve blueberry pancakes," said Homer, "a sweet roll, and a tall glass of orange juice."

The waitress jotted down Homer's order. "That's three orders of blueberry pancakes, a sweet roll, and a tall glass of o.j."

"I just want a glass of milk," said Henry.

"Large or small?"

"Small."

The waitress wrote it down and, taking their menus, left.

Homer said, "I'll be right back." He slipped out of the booth. "I'm just going to see if they have any good tacky postcards up by the cash register."

While Homer was gone, Henry flipped through the song selections on the small jukebox in the booth. He found two songs he wanted to listen to: "Only The Lonely" by The Motels and The Doobie Brothers' "Real Love." He dug his hand into his pocket, pulled out a quarter, and dropped it into the coin slot. He pushed the buttons E-7 and K-3. Then he took out his map to study it.

A minute later, Homer returned "Hey, look what I found!" Slipping into the booth, he handed Henry a postcard. "Now is that tacky, or is that tacky?" he demanded, perfectly delighted.

Henry examined the postcard. It showed a map of New Jersey, with all these little illustrations that told where there were great places to ski, hunt, fish, grow tomatoes, ride horses, lie by the ocean, and go sightseeing. At the top of the postcard it said: GREETINGS FROM NEW JERSEY. And just below it: The Garden State.

"That's pretty tacky," admitted Henry, handing him back the postcard.

Homer nodded proudly. He stuffed it into the breast pocket of his army jacket. "I really hit the jackpot. I got one for Nut and Bolt, too. I told the waitress to put it on our bill."

The waitress came with Homer's breakfast. Homer poured syrup over his stack of pancakes. Then he took a bite. His eyes lit up. "Say, these pancakes are delicious! Want some?"

"No thanks."

"You sure?" asked Homer. "You don't know what you're passing up." He tried his sweet roll. "Mmmm! Did I tell you I once worked in a place like this?"

"No."

"I was the cook. You sure you don't want some pancakes?"

"I'm sure."

"They're scrumptious. You sure you don't want just a bite?"

The thing was, Henry felt responsible for Homer. He was his pet, after all. He didn't want Homer to leave the table hungry.

"Positive," said Henry. "I don't know. I'm just not that hungry."

Homer still had a couple of pancakes left to eat, when he suddenly shoved the plate toward Henry. "Here," he ordered. "I want you to finish these." Then he announced that he was going to go back into the kitchen and congratulate the cook. Henry finished Homer's pancakes, and then the waitress came with the check. The waitress looked as if she wanted to kill Henry when he took out all his change. Henry left a small tip, and then counted his money. He only had a dollar and thirty-one cents left.

After what seemed like ages, the kitchen doors swung open, and Homer stepped out with the cook. The cook had his arm around Homer's shoulders, and he was laughing uproariously at something Homer had just said.

"Well, take it easy, buddy," the cook said to Homer and slapped him on the back.

Still Busy

"Guess what?" said Henry as they left the House of Pancakes parking lot and started walking along the highway shoulder.

"What?" asked Homer.

"Guess."

"You won the Who Am I Sweepstakes?"

"Now how could I've won that?"

"That was my next question."

"We're almost there," said Henry.

"Almost where?"

"Heather Callahan's house."

"Oh," said Homer. He sounded sort of sad. "Gee, we sure have had some fun together."

"Don't worry, Homer," said Henry. "Heather Callahan loves pandas."

"Henry?"

"Yeah?"

"You don't think we could give Heather Callahan something else, do you?" asked Homer. "Something a little less extravagant."

"But we've come all this way, Homer."

"I know. I know."

Homer suddenly stopped. "Ah . . . ah . . . ah . . . ah-chooooooooooo!" he sneezed.

Henry, stopping, looked at him. "You OK?" he asked with concern.

"I think so," said Homer. "Ah . . . ah . . . ah . . . ah-choooooooooo!"

"Gesundheit!" said Henry. He wished he had a Scooter Pie to give Homer.

"Ah . . . ah . . . ah . . . ah-chooooooooooo!"

"Gesundheit!"

"Ah . . . ah . . . ah . . . ah-chooooooooooo!"

"Gesundheit!"

"I don't know why I can't shake this cold," said Homer.

"Do you want to sit down?" asked Henry. They were right by an ice-cream stand that was closed for the season, but which still had a number of picnic tables standing out in front of it.

"I'll be OK," replied Homer. "I don't want to slow us up."

Henry felt badly now. "We're not in *that* big of a hurry."

Homer sniffled. "Ah . . . ah . . . ah . . . ah-chooooooooooo!"

"Gesundheit!"

"Ah . . . ah . . . ah . . . ah-choooooooooo!" he sneezed again, and sat down at a picnic table.

Henry sat down beside him. "How long have you had this cold?" he asked.

"Ever since I got here."

"You didn't have it over in the Himalayas?"

Homer shook his head. "No. I must have caught it on the plane."

For several minutes neither one of them spoke. Then Homer said, "Henry?"

Henry looked at him. "Yeah?"

"I have a confession to make."

"What's that?"

"I was only kidding about the Scooter Pies," he said. "I mean, about them curing colds."

Henry stared at him. "No!" he said.

"I'm afraid so."

"But I read they cure colds, too."

Homer looked at him in surprise. "You did?"

"In *Time* magazine."

"Really! Well, what do you know!"

"Ah, I'm only kidding," said Henry, casually.

"What?" cried Homer in astonishment.

"I'm only kidding," repeated Henry. "I know Scooter Pies don't cure colds."

"How long have you known?" demanded Homer. "How come you never said anything?"

Henry just shrugged. Then they both laughed.

"Well, I guess we should get going," said Henry finally.

Henry followed the map as best he could. They

walked along until they came to a traffic light, and then they turned down a quiet street lined with houses that you just knew had great kickball or whiffleball games on summer evenings.

Trudging along, they came to a big shopping mall. Homer spotted a telephone booth.

"Hey!" he cried. "There's another phone. Mind if I try calling my folks again?"

"But we spent almost all our money on breakfast," said Henry.

Homer's face fell. "Oh, we did?"

Henry felt sorry for him. "Listen," he said. "I can give you a dime, anyway. If you like, you can try calling them collect."

"Well, if you think so," said Homer, eagerly. "I mean, it doesn't make any difference to me if I call them or not."

For someone who it didn't make any difference to, Homer certainly crossed the parking lot in a big hurry. When they reached the phone booth, Henry gave Homer a dime and then sat down on the curb to wait.

Homer set down his suitcase, stepped into the phone booth, inserted his dime into the phone, and dialed O.

"Hello, operator," he said. "I'd like to make a collect call." He gave the operator the number he wanted to call and his name. Then, placing his paw over the mouthpiece, he said to Henry, "I'll just be two seconds."

There was a long pause as Homer listened to the receiver. Finally, he hung up. "It's still busy. The operator told me to try again in a few minutes," he added quickly.

A few minutes later, Homer tried again, but it was still busy. So he tried again a little bit later, but it was *still* busy.

"Who the heck's gabbing on the phone?" Homer demanded in exasperation. He hung the receiver up with a crash, then stepped out of the phone booth and sat down beside Henry.

"Ah . . . ah . . . ah . . . ah-chooooo!" sneezed Homer. "Ah . . . ah . . . ah . . . ah-choooooo! I don't believe this," he said miserably, handing Henry back his dime.

"Maybe they'll be off later," said Henry, who felt like it was all his fault that Homer was so depressed.

"I doubt it," replied Homer hopelessly.

After a minute passed, Henry was about to ask Homer if he was ready to get going, but then, glancing over at him, he changed his mind.

Homer's eyes had suddenly become very moist, and Henry was awfully worried that Homer was about to start crying.

A Great Idea

As it turned out, Homer just had to sneeze. "Ah
. . . ah . . . ah . . . ah-choooooooooo!"

Henry sighed with relief. "Let's go into the A & P.
Maybe they have something for colds." He stood up.

Sniffling, Homer got up and followed Henry into
the supermarket.

The moment they walked in, a clerk asked them to
leave their gear up in front of the store, by all the potted
mums and poinsettias that were for sale on the ledge
under the windows. Apparently, he was worried they
might try and walk out with something in their lug-
gage.

With Thanksgiving just a day away, the supermarket was having a big special on frozen turkeys. As they
were walking down the frozen foods aisle, Homer suddenly cried out, "Mildred!"

Practically everyone in the store heard him.

He rushed over to one of the frozen turkeys in the freezer, picked it up, and held it in his arms as if it was a baby.

"They butchered you!" he wailed, forlornly. "They butchered my poor pet turkey!" He was making quite a scene.

Henry stepped over to him and placed his arm around his shoulders. "It's OK, Stanley," he said, comfortingly. "We can get you another pet turkey. Really."

Homer looked at Henry with tears in his eyes. "You mean it?" he asked.

"Yes."

"One just like Mildred?"

"One just like Mildred."

Homer looked lovingly at the frozen turkey. Then he opened his eyes wide in horror. "They're not!" he cried in this very appalled voice. "I'm shocked! Shocked! They're only selling you for seventy-nine cents a pound? To me, Mildred, you're worth a thousand dollars a pound."

A big crowd had gathered around them.

"Now, Stanley, put the poor turkey down," said Henry. "And come along with me."

Homer delicately placed the turkey back into the freezer. He patted it gently. "She was such a good pet," he said.

"Yes, I know," said Henry, looking at all the people. "Now let's get going." He quickly led Homer away.

When they turned down the next aisle—the laundry detergents, paper towels, soaps, toilet paper, dishwashing lotions, dog food and cat food aisle—Henry and Homer cracked up. They walked down the aisle and turned up the fruits and vegetables aisle. At the end of the fruits and vegetables aisle, they found the magazine section.

Henry said, "I'll go ask someone where the stuff for colds is," and left Homer reading a *Spiderman* comic book.

When Henry arrived at the cash registers, he went to the one marked: EXPRESS LANE—10 ITEMS OR LESS, and got in line behind these two old women.

"Well," one of the women was saying. "I think it's just awful. Imagine. Murdering some poor fellow's pet turkey like that."

"There's so many cruel, heartless people who care only about themselves," said the other woman. "As long as they're happy, they think that's all that matters."

The other woman shook her head. "That's the problem with this world," she said. "Nobody cares about other people's feelings."

Henry felt terrible. He went over and sat down on the big pile of dog food bags by Aisle 2. He felt so ashamed of himself for giving Homer to Heather Callahan. He was just another of those cruel, heartless people who care nothing about anyone else's feelings but their own. While he sat there, Henry found himself staring at a sign hanging above the cash registers for a battery-operated kitchen knife to cut your Thanksgiving turkey with: IF YOU'RE NOT 100% SATISFIED, WE'LL GIVE YOU YOUR MONEY BACK—NO QUESTIONS ASKED.

Henry leaped up and went over to one of the ca-

shiers. "Where can I find the manager?" he asked.

"You looking for a job?" the cashier wanted to know.

"No. I have a complaint."

"Oh. He's probably over in his office," the cashier said, and pointed to a door marked MANAGER.

Henry walked over and knocked on the door.

"Come in," said a voice inside the office.

Henry opened the door.

"Hello, son," said a man with a red jacket and a black tie, who was sitting behind a big desk. There was a pin on the pocket of his jacket that said JIM MARTIN, and just underneath it, MANAGER. "What can I do for you?" he asked.

"I have a complaint."

"Don't tell me you want to complain about the turkeys, too!"

"No."

The manager let out an enormous sigh. "Whew!" he exclaimed. "You wouldn't believe all the women who've come in here in the last five minutes screaming about how I've been murdering pet turkeys."

"No!"

"What's this world coming to?" The manager shook his head. "Anyway, tell me," he said, with a smile. "What can I do for you?"

"I'd like to return a panda."

"We don't sell pandas," said the manager. "Frozen turkeys and chickens, yes. But no pandas."

"Oh, I didn't get him here," said Henry. "I sent away for him from the back of a box of cereal."

"Oh, I'm afraid we don't handle returns for merchandise offered on the back of cereal boxes," said the manager. "You'll have to deal with the company directly. I suggest you just send them back the panda. If the panda is still under guarantee, the cereal people will refund your money."

"But I can't wait that long," said Henry.

"I'm sorry," said the manager. "But there's nothing I can do."

Tears filled Henry's eyes. "But—but—but—you don't understand. . . ."

"Come on now," said the manager. "You're a big young man. Don't cry."

"But my parents will kill me if I bring him home. They told me to get rid of him—or else," screamed Henry, pretending to cry.

The manager looked as if he was about to cry himself. "You remind me a little of myself when I was your age," he said. "The panda isn't defective, is he?"

"He can't stop sneezing."

"Hmm. I see. And what kind of cereal was it?"

Henry told him.

"Tell you what . . ."

"Gilbert."

"Tell you what, Gilbert. Let me make a few phone calls. Maybe I can work something out."

"Really?" said Henry. Wiping a tear, he stepped out of the office and closed the door behind him. He leaned up against the employee time clock, and waited.

After a minute, the manager's door opened, and the manager stepped out, beaming. "Well, it's all arranged, Gil," he said, proudly. "You can return the panda here."

Henry broke into a big smile. "Yeah?"

The manager grinned. "They told us to just put him to sleep and send him back."

"Great!" said Henry. "I'll go get him."

Henry raced back to the magazine section, where he found Homer still reading the *Spiderman* comic book.

"Guess what?" cried Henry.

"What?" replied Homer, without looking up from his comic book.

"You're going home!"

Homer put down the comic book. "What are you talking about?"

"You're going home. I just arranged it. You're going back to the Himalayas."

Homer appeared stunned. "Are.you kidding?"

Henry could scarcely keep from laughing. "No! Honest!"

"Can you do that?" asked Homer. "I mean, what about my contract?"

"Forget the contract," said Henry, dismissing it with a wave of his hand. "I'm the owner, aren't I? I can return you if I want. Besides, who knows? I might even get my money back. You *were* defective after all."

"I was not!"

"What about all that sneezing"

"Geez, a guy can't even sneeze anymore." Homer grinned. "So when am I going?"

"Right now."

"I can't believe it!" said Homer. "I'm really going home." He let out a hoot. Then, growing serious, he said, "But what about Heather Callahan?"

"Don't worry about that."

All of a sudden Homer hugged Henry.

"Please!" said Henry, laughing. "Try to control yourself!"

A woman pushing a shopping cart stopped to stare at them.

"My long lost cousin," explained Homer.

"Be sure to sneeze a lot," instructed Henry as he led Homer to the manager's office. "I told him you have a bad cold."

They found the manager at his desk, writing. "Well, here's the panda."

"Ah . . . ah . . . ah . . . ah-choooooooooo!" sneezed Homer. "Ah-choooooooooo! Ah-choooooooooo! Ah-choooooooooo!"

"See what I mean?" said Henry.

"Ah-ah-ah-choooooooooo! Ah-choooooooooo! Ah-choooooooooo!"

The manager laid down his pen. "He certainly does sneeze a lot," he said, getting up.

"Ah-ah-ah-choooooooooo! Ah-choooooooooo! Ah-choooooooooo!"

"He hasn't stopped sneezing since I got him," explained Henry.

"Ah-ah-ah-choooooooooo! Ah-choooooooooo! Ah-choooooooooo!"

"Well," said Henry. "He's all yours."

"Ah-ah-ah-choooooooooo! Ah-choooooooooo! Ah-choooooooooo!"

"His sneezing is driving me crazy," said the manager. "No wonder your folks won't let you keep him."

"Ah-chooooooooooooooooooooooooooo!"

"I'll go get his suitcase," Henry said, and hurried out of the office.

Henry ran back into the main part of the supermarket and found the cookie aisle. After looking all over, he found the box he wanted. He brought it up to the EXPRESS LANE—10 ITEMS OR LESS—and paid for it with the last of his money. He got two cents change. Then, collecting Homer's suitcase, he walked into the manager's office, hiding the box behind his back.

"Could I have a minute alone with the panda?" Henry asked the manager.

The manager hesitated. "Well . . ." he said. "I guess so." He stepped reluctantly out and closed the door behind him.

"Here," Henry said to Homer. "I got you these." He gave Homer the box.

"*Scooter Pies!*" cried Homer.

"Look," said Henry, "why don't you keep the walkie-talkie I gave you. Sometimes on my shortwave radio I can get signals from all over the world. Who knows? Maybe the signal will carry across the Himalayas. If it does, we can keep in touch that way."

They shook. Henry opened the door to leave.

"Hey, Henry," said Homer.

Henry looked at him.

"Nothing," said Homer.

"What?"

"It's been real."

"Don't do anything I wouldn't do," said Henry, and stepped out.

Henry thanked the manager again, picked up his knapsack and left the store.

As he was crossing the parking lot, it occurred to Henry that there wasn't much point in continuing on to Heather Callahan's house without Homer. It seemed funny to just end the expedition this way. He had come so far. When he reached the street, he headed south, in the direction of home. He walked very, very slowly. He felt incredibly sad. He missed Homer.

One thing that made no sense at all to Henry was why they had to put Homer to sleep to send him home. Why couldn't he just stay awake? Something seemed awfully strange. Henry suddenly swung around and started running back to the mall.

Along with a Jiffy Cleaners, a K-Mart, a Bell Drugs, a Mr. Pizza, a bank with a drive-in window, and a barbershop, there was also a bookshop in the mall. Henry rushed in and, gasping for breath, asked to see the dictionaries.

"Is this for yourself?" asked the saleswoman behind the counter.

"Yes."

"Well, here's one I think you'll just love," she said and, walking over to a big display of dictionaries, showed him one. "It's got lots of nice pictures in it."

"Thanks," said Henry, and turned to the *S*'s. "Slave . . . sleazy . . . sleek," Henry said to himself. Flipping the page, he found *sleep*.

He quickly read the definition.

> **sleep** 1: a state of being at rest, in which consciousness is suspended and the body relaxes 2: a state resembling sleep 3: DEATH (*The veterinarian put the old dog to sleep.*); also—

113

Henry's heart stopped. His knees felt all wobbly and he was sure he was going to faint.

They were going to *murder* Homer!

Captured!

Henry ran out of the bookstore. Dodging in and out between people, he sprinted down the sidewalk as fast as he could to the A&P and flew into the supermarket. He didn't knock before entering the manager's office; he just barged right in. The manager was at his desk, adding things up on a calculating machine. He looked up with surprise.

"Where is he?" demanded Henry, close to tears. "I want him back!"

The manager stood up. He looked very uneasy. "What's the matter, Gil?"

"Where's Homer?"

"Homer?"

"The panda."

"He's already gone."

Henry's heart stopped. "Gone?"

"The vet just took him away."

Henry felt weak. "Oh, my word!" He couldn't speak for a moment, he was so worked up. "Where's the vet's office?"

"On Woodbury Street. Across the street from Golf Land."

Henry tore out of the A&P. In the parking lot, over by the mechanical bronco horse, a kid was popping wheelies on his Stingray bicycle. Henry ran over to him.

"Hey, kid," said Henry, excitedly. "Can I borrow your bike for a second?"

"Get out of here!" cried the kid.

"But I really need it," said Henry. "It's an emergency. A friend of mine's in big trouble."

"Borrow someone else's," said the kid.

Henry was all set to knock the kid off his seat and steal the bicycle. "Look," he said. "I'll give you five dollars if you let me borrow your bike."

"Five dollars!"

"Yeah," said Henry. "I only want to borrow it. What do you say?"

"Let's see the five dollars."

Henry suddenly remembered he was broke. "Wait," said Henry, digging into his knapsack. "I'll *give* you this if you just let me borrow your bike." He showed the kid his transistor radio. "It's worth twenty-five dollars easily." He gave it to him to see.

"You'll give this to me?" the kid asked, switching it on.

"Yeah."

116

"Plus five dollars?"

"No way!"

"Forget it then," said the kid, and clicked off the transistor radio.

"All right. All right," said Henry. "I'll give you the five dollars when I get back."

"Well . . ." said the kid, procrastinating.

"Come on," said Henry. "Don't be a jerk."

"All right," said the kid. He slid off the bicycle. "You better not break anything."

Henry hopped on the bicycle. He rode out of the mall parking lot, pedaling furiously. He zipped down the streets that he and Homer had taken that morning.

At the busy intersection of Route 30, Henry didn't have time to wait for the light to change. He looked both ways, saw he could make it if he was really quick, and rode over to the opposite side of the highway. With cars whizzing dangerously by him, he began riding along the highway in the direction of Golf Land.

As luck would have it, a patrol car pulled out of a nearby parking lot when Henry ran the light. The policeman swung out onto the highway and, siren wailing, signaled to Henry to pull over.

Henry had to think fast. He clutched the front of his sweatshirt pocket, where his walkie-talkie was stuffed.

"Quick! I've got to get to the vet's!" shouted Henry, frantically. He looked down at the big lump he was holding under his sweatshirt. "My pet gerbil is about to have babies!"

The policeman stared at the bulge in Henry's sweat-

shirt pocket. "Your pet gerbil is about to have babies?" he said with surprise.

"I've got to get her to the vet's across the street from Golf Land."

Evidently, Henry looked pretty desperate, for the policeman said, "Hop in the car. I'll drive you there."

While the policeman was putting the bicycle into the trunk of the patrol car, Henry, clutching the lump in his sweat shirt pocket, got into the back seat with his knapsack. The policeman sat down. "That wasn't a very smart thing to do," he said, as he pulled out onto the highway. "Whipping out into a dangerous intersection like that."

"I know," said Henry. "Normally I always wait for the light to change."

"You should *walk* your bicycle across the street."

"I usually do," replied Henry. "Honest."

"You were also riding against the traffic," continued the policeman. "You should ride with it."

"I know."

"How's the gerbil doing?"

Henry pretended to look at the gerbil. "She looks fine."

"What's her name?"

"Gladys."

The policeman was looking through his rearview mirror at Henry in a peculiar way. "You know something?" he said suddenly. "You look awfully familiar."

Henry turned and looked out his window. "I do?"

"I know I've seen you before."

"I look like a lot of kids."

119

"I know I've seen your face before."

"Everybody's always telling me that."

"What's your name?" asked the policeman.

"Who me?"

"Yeah."

"Jim."

"Jim what?"

"Jim Martin."

The policeman didn't say anything for a long time. He kept peering back at Henry through his rearview mirror. Henry felt very, very uneasy. His heart was racing.

"Um, I think you just passed the street the vet's on," said Henry, as he watched the street fly past the window.

The policeman said nothing.

Henry leaned forward in case the policeman hadn't heard him. "Excuse me, sir, but I think we missed the street."

The policeman didn't say a word. He just kept peering back at Henry through the rearview mirror. It was very scary.

"You can let me out anywhere," said Henry, nervously. "I can walk from here."

"The game's over, Henry," said the policeman sternly, and reached for the microphone on his police radio.

A Strange Rescue

"*Henry?* My name's Jim!" cried Henry.

"This is Lieutenant Parisi," said the policeman into the microphone. "I have the missing Whitfield boy. I'm bringing him into the station now."

Henry cried, "You can't bring me in! They'll kill him! They'll kill Homer!"

"You can stop playing games, Mr. Whitfield," said the policeman.

"But you don't understand!" exclaimed Henry. "They'll kill Homer if I don't stop them!"

"Who's Homer?"

"This panda."

"Listen, son. Don't you think you've played enough pranks on me?"

"But this isn't a prank! They'll really kill Homer if I don't stop them."

121

"Do you realize how much unhappiness you've caused your poor mom and dad?"

"You don't understand. I've got to save Homer! I've got to!"

"I understand more than you think," said the policeman and just drove on.

"Please can't we go to the vet's?" begged Henry. "Just for a minute?"

"No."

"Only *one* minute?"

"*No.*"

Henry pulled out his walkie-talkie. "Homer! Homer!" he cried into it. "It's a trick! A dirty rotten trick! They're going to kill you! Homer can you hear me? Run for your life! Homer? Homer? Are you there, Homer? Help, someone!"

But there was only a lot of static on the walkie-talkie. It was no use.

The policeman said, "You certainly do have quite an imagination."

Henry, looking out his window, suddenly started to cry. He couldn't help it.

"Tell me, son," said the policeman. "Where did you spend last night?"

Henry refused to speak.

"Where did you spend last night?" the policeman repeated his question.

Still nothing.

"I asked you a question, young man."

"In the woods."

"All by yourself?"

"Homer was with me."

122

"Who's Homer?"

"A panda."

"When I ask you a question, Mr. Whitfield, I want a straight answer."

Henry sighed. "OK. I was alone."

"Why did you run away?"

Henry wouldn't answer.

"I said, why did you run away?"

He still wouldn't speak.

"I asked you a quest—"

"To see this girl."

"Who?"

"No one you know."

"Don't get smart with me," the policeman told him. "I don't suppose it ever occurred to you, you could've gotten very lost? I tell ya, if you were my kid, I'd— Oh, my God!" The policeman suddenly slammed on his brakes.

As the police car screeched to a stop, Henry had just enough time to glance out the front of the windshield before he was thrown forward.

Lights flashing, the monsters' spaceship was hovering above the road, blocking their view.

The moment the car had stopped, Henry sat up. He was fine. He watched as the spaceship landed on the pavement just ahead of them.

"I don't believe this is happening to me!" whimpered the policeman, terrified. "I just don't believe it!"

The spaceship door slipped open, the ramp magically descended, and Mr. 11135-00128, looking ugly as ever, appeared in the doorway.

The policeman fainted.

Grabbing his knapsack, Henry hopped out of the car and ran up the ramp. "Quick!" he cried. "We've got to save Homer!"

Henry forgot to talk into his walkie-talkie, so he had to say it again. As the door was closing behind him and Mr. 11135-00128, Henry saw Mrs. 11135-00128 sitting in the passenger's seat. He waved to her.

"Where is he?" asked Mr. 11135-00128, climbing into the driver's seat. He began to turn dials, flick switches, pull levers, push buttons. They lifted off.

"Over by Golf Land," said Henry into his walkie-talkie. He set his knapsack down. "I guess you have to follow the highway back about—"

"I know where Golf Land is," said Mr. 11135-00128.

"Oh, that's right," said Henry, remembering.

Mr. 11135-00128 didn't follow the highway. He took the shortcut: over the woods and houses. It was quite a sight, seeing all the tiny trees and houses and lawns and streets and cars from the spaceship windshield. It felt very weird flying, too.

When they arrived over Golf Land, Henry pointed to a cluster of buildings and a parking lot just across the street. "That must be the vet's," he said into his walkie-talkie. "That's where Homer is."

"Darn it!" said Mr. 11135-00128, as he hovered the spaceship above the parking lot. "I don't see a parking spot."

"There's someone pulling out," said his wife, and pointed to a blue pickup truck that was backing out of a spot.

The moment the spaceship landed in the parking lot

and the door slid open, Henry raced out and dashed into the office that said ELIZABETH SCHWENK, D.V.M. in the window.

He burst into the reception room and went up to the receptionist, who was sitting at her desk, typing. "Where's Homer?" Henry demanded, looking about. The reception room was empty.

The receptionist stopped typing and peered at Henry through her glasses. "Homer?" she inquired.

"The panda you just brought in," said Henry. "I want him back!"

"Do you have an appoint—" the receptionist started to say, when she suddenly fainted.

Henry looked behind him. The monsters had just walked in the door.

"Wait here," Henry told them, speaking into his walkie-talkie. He opened the door that led into the back. He rushed down the corridor, opening all the doors. You could hear dogs barking everywhere. He found a big black Newfoundland dog caged up in one room. A terrier in another. A bunch of meowing cats in another room. But no Homer.

Finally, he came to a door that said OPERATING ROOM and opened it.

And there was Homer.

He was lying stretched out on an operating table, with nothing on and his arms at his sides.

And he lay absolutely still.

Henry's heart sank. He was too late.

The Experiment

Henry came over to the operating table and stood beside Homer. Enormous tears welled up in his eyes. It was terrible to see that big black and white body lying so still. Henry could hardly swallow.

Just then, Homer's eyelids opened a little bit—at least, Henry could've sworn they did.

"I must be seeing things," Henry told himself.

But a moment later, Homer's eyelids opened a little bit again, then closed.

Henry grinned. "Well, seeing as Homer is dead, I might as well take his I.D. bracelet." He reached over and undid the large silver bracelet from Homer's wrist.

"Hmm," Henry went on, curiously. "I wonder what made Homer Homer?" He picked up a scalpel from a nearby table that was covered with surgical tools. "I've always wanted to see the insides of a panda.

Let's see now . . . I guess I'll start by dissecting the heart."

Homer suddenly sat up. "Oh, no you don't!" he cried. "And give me back my I.D. bracelet!" He snatched the bracelet out of Henry's hand.

Henry pretended to look amazed. "Homer! You're alive!" he exclaimed.

"Some friend you are!" replied Homer, indignantly, putting on his I.D. bracelet. "I'm no sooner dead and you start pocketing my valuables."

"Look who's talking! Some friend *you* are!" said Henry. "Pretending you were dead."

"I just wanted to see what you'd do," said Homer. "How'd you know I wasn't dead?" He put on his sweater. "Did the vet tell you? She promised she wouldn't tell."

"I saw you open your eyes," said Henry. "How come you're not dead, anyway?"

"You sound real disappointed."

"Well?"

"Oh, the manager of the A&P called the vet and told her not to do anything to me," explained Homer, putting on his army jacket.

"He did?"

"He told the vet you were probably on your way over to get me," continued Homer. "So, I thought I'd do an experiment in human behavior. You know me."

"Some experiment."

"Oh, guess what?" said Homer. He hopped off the operating table.

"What?"

Homer picked up his hat and put it on. "I don't have a cold, after all."

"You don't?"

Homer shook his head. "No. I'm all cured. The vet said it must have been an allergy. Since I found out I'm going home, I've practically stopped sneezing."

"Great!"

Henry picked up Homer's suitcase, and the two of them walked out to the reception room. They found the monsters sitting in armchairs, in a pool of lamplight, reading magazines.

Mr. 11135-00128 looked up from his magazine. "All set?" he asked.

Henry nodded. "Everything's fine," he said, into his walkie-talkie. "Thanks a million for coming to the rescue."

The monster tossed his magazine onto a small table. "Glad to be able to help out," he said, standing up.

"Thank goodness we forgot our golf clubs and had to come back," said his wife. "Otherwise, we never would've heard you trying to warn Homer on your walkie-talkie." She got up and laid her magazine on the table.

"Well, you certainly came in the nick of time," said Henry into his walkie-talkie.

"Is there anything else we can do?" asked Mrs. 11135-00128.

"If it wouldn't be too much trouble," said Henry, "do you think you could give Homer a lift home to the Himalayas?"

Homer's face lit up.

"No trouble at all," said Mr. 11135-00128. "How about you, Henry? Can we give you a ride home, too?"

"That's okay. I'll walk home."

Outside in the parking lot, a crowd of people had gathered around the spaceship. The moment they saw the monsters they all fainted. Way off in the distance there was the wailing of a police siren. "Maybe you'd better drop me off somewhere else," Henry said to Mr. 11135-00128.

As they were walking up to the spaceship ramp, Homer waved to the unconscious crowd. "And if I'm elected . . ." he started to bellow out, when Henry pulled him inside the spaceship.

As the spaceship was lifting off, two patrol cars careened into the parking lot, lights spinning, sirens screaming. A bunch of policemen leaped out with rifles and began firing at them. The bullets bounced off the outside of the spaceship like spitballs.

"Shall I teach them a lesson?" asked Mr. 11135-00128, as he hovered the spaceship above them.

"Yeah, do!" cried Homer, excitedly, over his shoulder.

"No, don't!" said Henry quickly, into the walkie-talkie. "I'm in enough trouble."

When they were safely out of sight, Henry slipped on his knapsack. He told Mr. 11135-00128 that he could just let him out anywhere.

"Well, I guess this is good-bye," he said, sadly, to Homer.

"What do you think will happen when you get home?" asked Homer.

Henry shrugged. "I don't know," he said. "I'll probably have lots of explaining to do."

Homer nodded. "I've got a feeling I will, too." He pulled out a ballpoint pen and a small note pad from the pocket of his army jacket. He flipped open the note pad, and asked, "What's your address?"

Henry told him, then said, "I want yours, too."

Homer scribbled it down. "I still have your sleeping bag, you know," he said. He tore out the sheet of paper and gave it to Henry.

"Why don't you hold on to it?" said Henry, folding the paper. He put it into his back pocket.

They both looked at each other for a minute without speaking.

"Here," said Homer. "You can give this to Heather Callahan." He slipped off his I.D. bracelet and gave it to Henry. "Tell her a panda once owned it."

Henry stared at him in astonishment. "You're *giving* me your I.D. bracelet?" he cried.

"It won't be easy, but somehow I'll just have to live without it," said Homer, dramatically.

"Are you sure you want to give this away?"

"Positive."

"I don't want to take it from you if you really want it."

"That's *OK*," replied Homer. "After all, what are friends for?"

"I really appreciate it, Homer," said Henry, putting the bracelet into his pocket. "Thanks a million." He paused. "Well . . ." He stuck out his hand.

Homer grabbed it, and said, "Hi, I'm a lumberjack!" He began to pull Henry's arm back and forth, back and forth, as if he were sawing wood.

Henry laughed. "Hey, I'm from the heart association," he said, and squeezed Homer's paw, then loosened his grip, then squeezed again, then loosened his grip again, so it felt like a pumping heart.

Homer pulled his paw away. "Where'd you pick this guy up from?" he cried, looking over at the monsters.

Mr. 11135-00128 brought the spaceship down in a deserted playground. Henry thanked the monsters once again and said good-bye. Then he stepped over to the door. Homer stood at the top of the ramp and watched as Henry walked down the ramp.

At the bottom of the ramp, Henry turned and gazed up at Homer. Homer looked as if he were about to cry. Henry tried to speak, but there was a lump in his throat. Finally, after almost a minute, he managed to say, "Well, take it easy."

"Hey, Henry," called Homer.

"Yeah?"

"Nothing."

"What?"

"Don't do anything I wouldn't do."

Henry smiled. "It's been real!" he shouted, and stepped onto the grass.

As the ramp was slipping back into the spaceship, Homer suddenly yelled, "I'll send you some tacky postcards from the Himalayas!" The spaceship door

slid closed, and then, with its lights spinning around and around, the spaceship lifted up into the air. With an enormous blast, it soared off, disappearing quickly into the darkening evening sky.

1620 Whippoorwill Road

Henry walked across the lawn of the playground toward a bunch of houses. He felt so lonely. It was growing darker by the minute. And cold, too. It seemed like years had passed since he'd left home yesterday morning.

As he was cutting across a deserted football field, Henry made up his mind that he was going to find the Callahans' house and give Heather Callahan the I.D. bracelet. "I'll only hate myself if I don't," he thought.

After Henry reached the end of the playground, he crossed a street, and walked over to a pool of light underneath a streetlamp. He began to take out his map, when he noticed, down at the corner of the block, a street sign that said WHIPPOORWILL ROAD.

"Well, what do you know," said Henry.

As Henry walked along Whippoorwill Road,

checking each house number, he noticed that some of the houses had Thanksgiving decorations. One house had crayon drawings of turkeys taped up on the living room window. In the living room window of another house, there was a bunch of cutout Pilgrims standing around with some Indians. All the Pilgrims and Indians were smiling—it looked as if somebody had just told a great joke.

"I guess the Pilgrims were on a sort of expedition, too," Henry said to himself.

When Henry arrived at 1620 Whippoorwill Road, he stopped before the house. It was a yellow house with white trim and lots of bushy shrubs growing along the front of the house. The windows of the house were all glowing with light. Curtains with little pandas on them were hanging in two of the upstairs windows.

Heather Callahan's bedroom.

Suddenly, a grandfather clock began to chime in the front hallway. Henry counted the chimes. Five. It was five o'clock already!

"Oh, this is stupid," Henry said to himself.

Taking a deep breath, he marched resolutely up the flagstone steps to the front door, hesitated, then rang the doorbell.

Staring at the husk of Indian corn that was tacked up on the front door, Henry could feel his heart pounding.

After a moment, the porch light snapped on and then the front door opened, and Henry found himself looking at Mrs. Callahan. She was wearing blue dishwashing gloves. She opened the storm door. "Hello," she said, cheerfully.

"Hello," said Henry. "Is Heather in?"

"She should be," said Mrs. Callahan. "Come on in." She held the storm door open for him.

"Thank you," said Henry, stepping inside.

Mrs. Callahan walked over to a carpeted staircase that led up to the living room. "Heather!" she called.

A girl's voice answered, "What?"

"There's a young man here to see you!"

"Who is it?"

"Just come downstairs, please," said Mrs. Callahan. She turned to Henry. "Sit down. Sit down. For heaven's sake, make yourself comfortable. I'm Heather's mom."

"I'm a friend of Heather's from school," said Henry, unslinging his knapsack. He sat down in a chair by the grandfather clock.

Mrs. Callahan stepped over to the stairs again. "Oh, *Heather,*" she called.

The girl's voice replied, rather impatiently, "*I'm* coming!"

Mrs. Callahan smiled at Henry. "*Some*body's in a cranky mood," she said. She bent down and picked up a roll of paper towels and a can of Pledge that were sitting on one of the steps. "Is your mom all ready for Thanksgiving tomorrow?" she asked.

"I don't think so."

Mrs. Callahan shook her head. "Me neither. We're having some relatives over, and I've got tons of cleaning left to do." She sighed. Then she glanced up the stairs. "*That* girl," she said, shaking her head. "*Heather!*" she called again.

"I said I'm coming!"

Smiling, Mrs. Callahan looked at Henry. "She'll be down in just a sec. Well. It was awfully nice to meet you," she said, and disappeared into another room.

The moment Henry was alone, he pulled out Homer's I.D. bracelet. It sure felt funny to be in Heather Callahan's house. The grandfather clock was *tick-tock*ing loudly.

"*Henry?*" said a girl's voice suddenly, over by the stairs.

Henry turned, saw Heather Callahan, and leaped to his feet. She looked so pretty. Henry absently stuck the I.D. bracelet into his pocket.

"Hello, Heather," squeaked Henry.

Heather Callahan came down the stairs. "What are you doing here?" she asked. "Everybody's looking all over for you."

Henry nervously put his hands into his pockets. "Oh, yeah?"

Heather Callahan said, "I thought you were dead."

Henry pulled his hands out of his pockets. "You did?"

"I was so upset."

Henry could scarcely believe his ears. "You were?"

"Well, I thought you were dead," she said. "You're on the front page of today's newspaper, you know."

Henry pretended to be astonished. "*Me?*"

"You seem different. Where have you been? Where did you sleep last night?"

"In the woods."

Heather Callahan's eyes opened wide. "You slept in the woods? Weren't you scared?"

"Naaa," replied Henry.

"Why'd you run away?" she asked. "Don't you know how worried everyone is?"

Henry was quiet for a moment. "I didn't mean to worry anybody."

"Why'd you run away?"

Henry hesitated, then mumbled something.

"What?"

Henry's eyes fell to the floor. "To come here."

Heather Callahan looked very surprised. "*Here?* Why'd you come here?"

"I don't know. To see you."

"But you see me all the time in school."

"I know. But I've never talked to you. Besides, I had something—"

"You could've just called me."

"I could've?"

"Of course," she said. "My gosh! I can't believe you went through all this just to see me."

The way she said it made Henry feel sort of stupid. It wasn't working out quite as he hoped. "Listen," he said. "I wonder if I could borrow your phone for a minute? I want to call my mom and dad and then I'll get going."

Heather Callahan looked at him like he was crazy. "But you just got here!" she cried. "Don't you want something to eat? You must be starving!"

"No thanks," replied Henry.

"Won't you eat *some*thing?"

"Well . . ."

"Please?"

"Actually," said Henry. "You wouldn't happen to have any Scooter Pies, would you?"

It wasn't until later, after he'd called home, that Henry remembered the I.D. bracelet. He suddenly thought of it as, sitting at the Callahan's kitchen table, he was telling Heather Callahan about the cereal box offer for the panda. He began to pull the I.D. bracelet out of his pocket, when Heather Callahan said, "You got me a panda, too! You're something else, Henry Whitfield. Look. Would you promise me one thing?"

"What's that?" asked Henry.

"Would you promise me you'll wait until I get to school on Monday before you start telling all the other kids how you ran away? I want to be there, too. OK? Please?"

Henry smiled. "Sure," he said, and put the I.D. bracelet back into his pocket. He decided not to give her the bracelet, after all. He didn't need to. Instead, he thought he would just send it back to Homer in the Himalayas. To make sure it didn't get lost en route, he thought he should send it by Special Delivery—with maybe a really tacky postcard or two stuck inside the package for good measure.